DON'T WHISPER
TOO MUCH

&

PORTRAIT OF
A YOUNG ARTISTE
FROM BONA MBELLA

The Griot Project

Series Editor: Carmen Gillespie, Bucknell University

This book series, associated with the Griot Project at Bucknell University, publishes monographs, collections of essays, poetry, and prose exploring the aesthetics, art, history, and culture of African America and the African diaspora.

The Griot is a central figure in many West African cultures. Historically, the Griot had many functions, including as a community historian, cultural critic, indigenous artist, and collective spokesperson. Borrowing from this rich tradition, the *Griot Project Book Series* defines the Griot as a metaphor for the academic and creative interdisciplinary exploration of the arts, literatures, and cultures of African America, Africa, and the African diaspora.

Expansive and inclusive in its appeal and significance, works in the *Griot Project Book Series* will appeal to academics, artists, and lay readers and thinkers alike.

Titles in the Series:

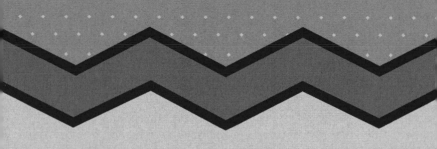

FRIEDA EKOTTO

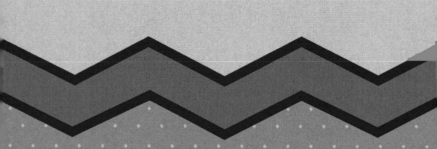

DON'T WHISPER TOO MUCH

Translated by
CORINE TACHTIRIS

PORTRAIT OF A YOUNG ARTISTE FROM BONA MBELLA

Bucknell | BUCKNELL
UNIVERSITY | UNIVERSITY
PRESS

Lewisburg, Pennsylvania

Library of Congress Cataloging-in-Publication Data

Names: Ekotto, Frieda, author. | Tachtiris, Corine, translator. | Ekotto, Frieda. Chucote pas trop. English. | Ekotto, Frieda. Portrait d'une jeune artiste de Bona Mbella. English.
Title: Don't whisper too much : and Portrait of a young artiste from Bona Mbella / by Frieda Ekotto ; translated by Corine Tachtiris.
Description: Lewisburg : Bucknell University Press [2019] | The publication of this translation brings the English-speaking world two path-breaking works by Frieda Ekotto—the novel Chuchote pas trop (Don't Whisper Too Much) and the short story collection Portrait d'une jeune artiste de Bona Mbella (Portrait of a Young Artiste from Bona Mbella). | Includes bibliographical references.
Identifiers: LCCN 2018029539 | ISBN 9781684480272 (cloth) | ISBN 9781684480289 (pbk.)
Subjects: LCSH: Lesbians—Africa—Fiction.
Classification: LCC PQ3989.3.E36 A2 2019 | DDC 843/.92—dc23
LC record available at https://lccn.loc.gov/2018029539

A British Cataloging-in-Publication record for this book
is available from the British Library.

♾ The paper used in this publication meets the requirements of the American National Standard for Information Sciences—Permanence of Paper for Printed Library Materials, ANSI Z39.48-1992.

www.bucknell.edu/UniversityPress

Distributed worldwide by Rutgers University Press

Manufactured in the United States of America

CONTENTS

A NOTE ON THE TRANSLATION

CORINE TACHTIRIS

The fact of women loving women is more easily emphasized grammatically in French since nouns, adjectives, and other parts of speech are gendered. I have tried to bring this into the translation by experimenting at times with grammatical gender in English. I owe the neologism lovhers to Barbara Godard's translation of Nicole Brossard's *Amantes*.

Duala words in the French are generally italicized only the first time they appear in the translation. Some are not italicized at all in recognition of the multilingual nature of the stories' settings, of the text itself, and the world in which we live. English words italicized in the French generally remain in italics in the translation.

The goals and strategies of the translation are described in greater detail in my article, "Giving Voice: Translating Speech and Silence in Frieda Ekotto's *Don't Whisper Too Much*," *Translation Review* 98, no. 1 (2017): 49–64.

INTRODUCTION

"In the Flow of Whisperings"

LINDSEY GREEN-SIMMS

The publication of this translation brings the English-speaking world two path-breaking works by Frieda Ekotto—the novel *Chuchote pas trop* (*Don't Whisper Too Much*) and the short story collection *Portrait d'une jeune artiste de Bona Mbella* (*Portrait of a Young Artiste from Bona Mbella*).

Don't Whisper Too Much takes place in a Fulani village in Northern Cameroon and revolves around three generations of mothers and daughters who break taboos by intimately loving other women. The main love story involves Ada, an orphan who seeks to know the story of her mother, and Siliki, an older disabled woman who has chosen to live on the village outskirts. All seven stories in *Portrait of a Young Artiste from Bona Mbella* take place in Bona Mbella, a neighborhood of Cameroon's largest city Douala, and most feature the young lesbian Chantou. Stylistically, the two works are quite different. *Whisper* reads like a haunting prose poem with ambiguous speakers, flashbacks, and fragmented journal excerpts. *Portrait*, much in the style of Jean-Pierre Bekolo's *Quartier Mozart* (a film adored by Chantou) and Patrice Nganang's *Dog Days*, makes use of urban Cameroonian dialogue, gossip, and irreverent humor. But what both works have in common is the compulsion to "open the breach onto new stories" (*Portrait*), to make space for voices who have gone unheard, and to bring to the center the marginalized stories of women who love women.

At the heart of Ekotto's writing, which impressively ranges from fiction to scholarship to activism and often artfully blurs the lines between all three, lies a preoccupation with the related themes of confinement and of silence. In an interview with Beti Ellerson, Ekotto says, "Despite leaving the continent and becoming a scholar and professor, I too have felt confined. I have wanted to spill out, but I could not because I felt tied up everywhere. The first challenge I have encountered is language and its poetics as limits of representation when it comes to human experience." Born in the town of Yaoundé, Cameroon, Ekotto spent her young adult years in Switzerland before moving to the United States for university. Despite being in a relatively privileged position, however, it is not always easy to write as an African lesbian or about African lesbians. The imprecisions and impossibilities of language—including those that make the term "lesbian" difficult to apply to many African women who love women—mean that identity often evades easy representation and that the profundity and complexity of human experience often remain enigmatic. But what is also implicit here is that language is tied to power, and the inability to speak (or what Ekotto calls being "tied up") is, as Gayatri Spivak argues, an inability to be heard within hegemonic discourse.[1]

For Ekotto, then, confinement has to do with one's relation to systems of power. As she explains to Naminata Diabate, "Confinement is a serious issue for me—and it is not just the confinement of being behind closed doors or in prisons or whatever. What I call confinement is the impossibility of feeling free, of being able to participate in the world without feeling constrained by one's race, one's gender, one's sexual orientation etc. In a sense you're never free to do what you want because of all the outside forces that control you and control everything else."[2] Writing, then, allows Ekotto to carve out spaces within this confinement to "pierce the imperceptible layer of the unsayable and slide through the cracks" (oo). Though it was difficult to find a publisher willing to publish the subversive *Don't Whisper Too Much*, Ekotto persisted for ten years until the novel was eventually picked up in 2001 by Editions A3, a small publishing house in France, and then reprinted in 2005 by L'Harmattan, who also later published *Portrait* in 2010. Thus, even the publication history bears the traces of confinement and the difficulty of breaking through power structures.

As an activist, Ekotto speaks out against the silence imposed upon LGBTI people in sub-Saharan Africa where, in many countries, homosexuality has been increasingly criminalized and violence against LGBTI individuals has been on the rise. As perhaps the first openly lesbian Francophone African fiction writer and a unique voice in the Cameroonian intellectual community, Ekotto writes for and in solidarity with her gay family members, LGBTI activists across the continent, and gay compatriots who have lost their lives because of who they have loved.[3] And yet in her fiction, especially in *Don't Whisper Too Much*, silence takes on a more dialectical role. Silence is indeed tied to confinement, enclosure, and erasure, but it can also be a form of resistance and solidarity. For instance, when Ada first encounters Affi, the daughter of her lover Siliki who is literally confined in a *boui-boui* with other girls awaiting their wedding days, Ekotto writes: "Silence unites them, a silence that reaches the bottom of every chasm, the abyss of bitter anguish. Fear was fortifying their internal energies. Speech was emanating from silence. Doesn't muteness remain a useful form of resistance, even if it's humiliating?" (oo). Later in the novel, this spirit of silence is echoed in the story Siliki tells about her wedding night. Siliki tells Ada that despite the fact that the village gossips were listening in, she refused to make a sound on that first night of unwanted consummation: "Juicy gossip was limited, and no one could believe this drama: the defeat that my husband had just suffered. . . . The music of bodies was muffled in the silence of that night veiled by violence. The absence of crude moans represents a failure of the man's virility" (oo). Though silence is also undone with the very act of Siliki's narration and with the insistence on the women in the novel writing and reading each other's stories, Ekotto reminds us that "with Siliki, silence signifies the grandeur of her spirit" (oo). In other words, *Don't Whisper Too Much* emphasizes the fact that the voices that are lost or muffled are just as elegant and powerful as those that are retained.

Moreover, Ekotto's fiction often enacts its own silence by refusing to be immediately accessible and knowable. As Diabate writes of the novel, "Ekotto's style resists the facile consumption, digestion, and possible disposability of her narrative, thereby establishing the relationship between writing, sexuality, and resistance. The difficulty of telling who is speaking in the novel through the use of multiple and often undistinguished speakerly and writerly voices [as well as] the multiple ellipses and unfinished sentences . . . seem to reveal that the subversion of sexual norms is encoded through the subversion of textual norms."[4] And even in the more collo-

quial prose of *Portrait of a Young Artiste from Bona Mbella*, there seems to be a connection between sexual transgression and the complex interplay between the spoken and unspoken. For instance, Chantou recounts the story of her childhood friend Munyengue Kongossa (kongossa literally means gossip) who returns to Bona Mbella from abroad with a blond Mohawk, a visible sign of her queerness. She roams the neighborhood (referred to in the stories as "the quat," which is short for the French *quartier*), but "no one wants to talk to her because, as they say, you should think everything that you say but not say everything that you think" (oo). But the gossiper Munyengue Kongossa is far from being silenced, and the title of the story, "The Revenant," (which means both ghost and the one who returns) implies that like other ghosts Munyengue Kongossa, discernibly and unabashedly queer, returns to make visible that which has been repressed.[5] Left with few other options, Munyengue Kongossa eventually finds other forms of speech: she belches herself into existence.

In both *Whisper* and *Portrait*, voices insist on being heard, but often in cacophonous or undistinguishable ways. Speaking, in other words, does not seem to be the remedy for silence; it does not immediately get one out of the bind of confinement. Rather, speech and silence seem to be permanently intertwined: both can convey meaning, both can convey confusion, and both can be either tools of oppression or tools of resistance. As Ekotto says, "In the flow of *chuchotements*, (whisperings) there are too many voices. . . . Whatever voice you can catch is the one you follow."[6] Ekotto's writing therefore reflects the fragmentation and chaos of subjects who, like herself, want to spill out but feel tied up everywhere. This is perhaps why imagination is so important in both texts. In *Don't Whisper Too Much* Ekotto writes of Siliki and Affi, "Not a day goes by without mother and daughter journeying to far-flung lands where entire islands open up to greet them. Only imagination guarantees such transcendence. Only it provides ways to live the contradiction of consenting to another form of presence" (00). In the short story "The Movie Screen" Chantou's friend Miss Bami turns her home into an imaginary cinema where the children of the neighborhood play and act out their favorite films. At the end of the story, Miss Bami says, "Imagination, my dear, imagination is learning to create when you lack the means!" (00). What Ekotto's fiction provides, then, is the site for imagination, for prying open the universe of the possible, and for allowing the chaotic whisperings to flow more freely.

NOTES

1. See Beti Ellerson, Interview, "Frieda Ekotto: For an Endogenous Critique of Representations of African Lesbian Identity in Visual Culture and Literature," *African Women in Cinema Blog*, November 13, 2013, http://africanwomenincinema.blogspot.com/2013/11/frieda-ekotto-for-endogenous-critique.html (accessed November 27, 2015). In her interview with Naminata Diabate, Ekotto expressed that she prefers the term "women who love women," a phrase that allows for the multiplicity of experiences and expressions of African same-sex love between women and that does not presume Western identity categories. ("From Women Loving Women in Africa to Jean Genet and Race: A Conversation with Frieda Ekotto," *Journal of the African Literature Association (JALA)* 4, no. 1 [2009]: 181–203). However, in a recent personal communication,

Ekotto told me that she herself identifies as a Cameroonian lesbian and thinks of her novels and short stories as "queer."

2. Diabate, "From Women Loving Women in Africa," 183.

3. See both her interviews with Diabate and Ellerson for a discussion of her writing for family members struggling to come out (see n1 above). Ekotto has also spoken publicly about the death of her gay cousin in Cameroon and has written poignantly about figures such as Roger Jean-Claude Mbede, a gay man left to die after he was imprisoned in Cameroon for sending a love message to another man ("Why Do We Always Say Nothing?" paper delivered at the Modern Language Association Convention, Boston, MA, January 2013).

4. Naminata Diabate, "Genealogies of Desire, Extravagance, and Radical Queerness in Frieda Ekotto's *Chuchote Pas Trop*," *Research in African Literatures* 47, no. 2 (2016): 46–65.

5. As Avery F. Gordon writes of the ghost, "What is distinctive about haunting is that it is an animated state in which a repressed or unresolved social violence is making itself known, sometimes very directly, sometimes obliquely" (*Ghostly Matters: Haunting and the Sociological Imagination*, 2nd ed. [Minneapolis: University of Minnesota Press, 2008], xvi).

6. Diabate, "From Women Loving Women in Africa," 183.

DON'T WHISPER
TOO MUCH

PORTRAIT OF
A YOUNG ARTISTE
FROM BONA MBELLA

DON'T WHISPER
TOO MUCH

For my sister, Mirabelle Ekotto

AFFI, OR THE COMMUNION OF BODIES

Affi's mother had never learned the story of her own mother or grandmother, and that ignorance would later follow her daughter, the indelible sign of a persistent, shadowy fate.

In the village, they often evoked Affi's grandmother but rarely her mother. The latter murmured to herself in the deep complicity of the night. All the odors Affi and her mother had secreted since the day the Good Lord had ordained the girl's arrival on earth, well now, they became incrusted in the mat that Affi's mother wanted her to carry off like a treasure. More than that: as the sole proof and final keepsake of their intimacy . . .

Huddled in her mother's arms, Affi daydreams, still and silent, scarcely listening to the diffuse sound of the vague words her mother whispers like a prayer:

"Which star will shine for me and save my pearl, shelter her from time? I have no idea, and anyway, it doesn't matter. She's snug in my arms, where I want her to stay forever."

At that moment, something inexplicable manifests itself in the connection between Affi and her mother. The girl shivers suddenly. Her head is raised by an irresistible force, and she moves her mouth closer, brushing her mother's chin with her forehead. Their lips meet in a kiss of uninterrupted violence. The rusty steel ring adorning the mother's lower lip opens and catches on Affi's tongue. A warm, salty liquid trickles from the girl's mouth. Holding her tighter and tighter in her arms, the mother continues her whispering:

"My blood and yours mix like two lovhers *signing a pact of union, a carnal contract linking life to death. Your little hands, covered with henna, seek mine in a gesture of friendship, of human warmth between two bodies.*

"Make your shadow appear, make your fellow creature solidify there like a stamp of belonging. Your star is part of chaos; it shines only in the silent shadows. Oh my pearl, how I love you. I'll be with you always. You'll see, nothing will ever harm you."

Affi feels protected in her mother's arms. What she knows best about her mother is the spicy odor of her body at its boiling point. Its perfumes float into the air, diluted by the humidity of the night. This aroma will always be a part of Affi. It gives her the illusion that she is still swimming in her mother's amniotic fluid, something like a second birth. Here in the dark of night when the strangest sounds intermingle, when birds of ill omen beat their wings beneath the foliage, wild beasts wade in the vase of backwater, and perhaps, the spirits of the dead grow listless beneath their tombs—is it really possible to sleep?

Affi loses all sense of reason. Everything escapes her gaze, even her own body. These odors alone awaken her senses and intoxicate her, and these moments of intensity, of complicity between daughter and mother, transpire in perfect harmony, as if synchronized by a will to which they can only submit.

Affi often thinks of all those rites, all the customs of the village in which young girls are packed into a lightless hovel to await the fatal moment when they will be opened to life. It's an honorable day for the parents, docile and submissive to the traditions. What can these people do? The weight of tradition crushes them. They're just poor souls dazzled by the gifts of the man who has opened their daughter to life. That suits some of them just fine, obsessed as they are by the idea of marrying their children off to rich men who manage their multiple wives like they do their common goods. Nubile, alone in that night in which blood will trickle from exfoliation, the slivers of their hymens—sharpened by anger, as keen as a blade—will be their only weapon of defense, a useful and necessary protection for their bodies against all other physical violence. The most arduous discipline is practiced upon the young girls' bodies, bodies conjugated in all the tenses of silence. The mind, a perfect medium between earth and sky, stays where it is, lost in the ignorance of lowly parents. No one attends to the survival of the mind, neglected in the shadows, far from all reality. Only the abused body makes material the presence of this living, moving object.

◆◇◆

"Listen to my silent messages, symphony of my tenderness. Clarity of my wellspring, opacity of clouds. The evaporated music of my ashes now stirred and rekindled by the memory of an existence on fire. Yes, my daughter, my tinder-wood tree, rekindle me. Revive me with the spark of beautiful, brilliant, sun-drenched days. My budding star, de-petalled before knowing what it is to bloom. How could I lose you when you are my sun, when your rays warm the skin of my aged body, still laboring nonetheless along this toilsome path, a symbol of my duty as a woman of the village. The shadow on your eyelids melts slowly, asking me to join you in suffering. Forgive me for making you my final redemptive alibi. One day, you'll understand this sad

smile shrouding my woman's lips. How could I forget you, you, my only consolation? Don't cry—you have no more tears. Remember, your tears flowed in an immense bluish ocean where sharks and the bodies of the disappeared sway in the wild, enraged waves. You were born healthy, before the fetishes of the village women. You washed yourself in magic water. You're out of danger. You will not be tainted. Neither misfortune nor suffering will touch you."

◆◇◆◇◆

The mother and daughter's existence is the object of malicious gossip here. Affi's mother feels like she's being observed, disrobed, strip-searched by the eyes of the community. She ought to adopt an appropriate attitude, somewhere between servile humility and unwarranted pride, tolerate the gossip of some, the scandalmongering of others. But Affi's mother scorns that kind of intrigue. Her complicity with her daughter grows. Not a day goes by without mother and daughter journeying to far-flung lands where entire islands open up to greet them. Only imagination guarantees such transcendence. Only it provides ways to live the contradiction of consenting to another form of presence. Stirred by the fruits of her dream, Affi's mother shifts her body. She turns the mat over, changes position to rest her back, strained from her daily labor. She remains huddled there, until the early hours when the morning cockcrows wrench her from restorative sleep.

◆◇◆◇◆

Affi's mother must overcome a double contradiction: the people around her and her own self. She must go beyond thought, beyond silence, dominate them so that, perhaps, another form of conception may be born, the only truth that consciousness is capable of registering. The kind of thought that verges on the forbidden, even if it's meant to be blunt and ungrateful. Sobbing over the shadows of her fate is a lost cause—this is her maxim—a despair with no more fear. Of anything. Not even death . . .

In the face of this catastrophe, courage pervades Affi's mother and guides her emotions wisely. Not a single word must slip out. Silence permeates every relationship. Affi's mother has no right to violate the secret. She cannot tell her daughter what fate awaits her. And so whispering words becomes a means, one possible opening to the quest. Yet finding a way to transmit the message to her daughter is no simple task for her. In the Fulani village, speaking isn't always easy. There is so much that is forbidden.

◆◇◆

Affi's mother is tall, seemingly ageless, with a beauty that has always unsettled the local Fulani men. Her pagne skirt, tightly knotted around her waist, highlights a backside whose firm, exaggerated undulations perhaps mistakenly confirm a taste for licentiousness. People often wonder how she has withstood the decrepitude that most of the women here succumb to after giving birth to a child. It's unthinkable that she could be a mother. Her skin shows no sign of slackening. Her athletic legs remain as slender and nimble as a young girl's. You could easily take her not for Affi's mother but her older sister. She has worn a plate in the form of a trapezoid on her lower lip since she was fifteen and has a fine-featured face with various kinds of jewelry around her long neck. And her breasts, despite the fact that she nursed Affi, are steely . . .

From birth, Affi had become accustomed to her mother's saliva as she lengthily licked her like a wild beast with its little one. Her tongue—agile, gentle, pointed—spread a saliva whose taste would soon have no secrets for the little girl. The sensation of that pink flesh on her body sent Affi into a state of extreme beatitude. She would not grow drowsy until after the ritual she so jubilantly awaited. Even with her eyes closed, when her mother's tongue traveled over her fragile body, Affi felt it, like the fringe of a salty wave brushing her skin and leaving in its wake an inexpressible sensation. She writhed languorously during each session to show the infinite pleasure the maternal tongue gave her.

◆◇◆

Affi's mother is nevertheless affected by how others view her relationship with her daughter, who now stays glued to her. Women, inseparable from darkness in this part of the world, give birth in pain. The mother often thinks how easy it is to slip into the mold of tradition without, however, respecting it. The complexity of the situation doesn't escape her. Why question her ancestors, tradition? It's a knot that Affi's mother could untangle, if she took the time to put her mind to work—only the light of her mind can come to her aid against the doubt now haunting her.

Everything around her begins to seethe with motion. Something like a new chapter is beginning. Her head is where the work finally begins. She's bubbling on the inside and preparing to blow off the lid. Caught up in the whirlwind of emotions, she thinks, bemusedly, about her dead mother who lived through the same events with resignation. Affi's mother questions everything, even herself, and everything her mother instilled in her by accustoming her to these tongue baths. In Fulani tradition, young girls are torn from their mothers at birth and immediately entrusted to the people for their traditional education. The custom is sacred and wise, but deep down, she still protests. Indeed, when it comes to her daughter, her pearl, the stakes change—it's a question of her blood. The tradition's continuation must be ensured, the same as the people's day-to-day survival. But for the Fulani, who is "the people"? Men are its key representatives; women and children are excluded. Secretly, Affi's mother blesses her daughter, places a star over her, over each girl birthed by a village woman in twofold pain. From that moment on, the mother no longer exists. Her mission accomplished, her life is of no more interest until the next delivery. Affi's mother refuses to think about the moment when they will take her, her own daughter, this child that she kept in the hollow of her belly, delicate fruit of her body . . .

Word after word, Affi's story reconstructs the genesis of her mother's and grandmothers' story, the story of all Fulani women, and so on and so forth in a bloodied ballet troupe. Maybe the moment for the rift in memory is slowly approaching its irruption.

"Affi, my sunshine, during your captivity, whatever you do, don't get distracted. Confinement is a constant in life—better to recognize it and ask yourself the best way to come to terms with the kind confronting you. The other is our enclosure from time immemorial: there is both the impossibility of staying confined within ourselves and the difficulty of facing this other. We

live enclosed in our own envelope as well the other's envelope. Even the enclosure of time is burdensome. Enclosure, confinement, captivity, command—just words to explain the despair in which you find yourself in the deep of nights where silence reasons. Escape, sure, but what conditions must be met to break out successfully? Please remain calm and be obedient. I don't want any misfortune to befall you, my sunshine. You're my sunshine. If you remain very calm, as calm as the sea before the waves invade, you'll hear those distant waves approach, the ones that will bring you the depth and inspiration to survive that indignation. In an enclosed space, time is plentiful. You know, it's said the sun never completely disappears. We feel like it's left us when we shiver with cold but it returns unexpectedly, bathes our feet in light and warms our heart. Remember, my sunshine, you'll never disappear completely. My legacy to you is a lever that will let you lift mountains."

◆◇◆

Affi was bathed in this way by her mother's saliva up until the night of her capture by the Fulani men. That gentle tongue traversed her body like a warm shower, a source of inexhaustible bounty, a launch of hope, pain both bitter and sweet. The fragrant perfume of her mother's saliva pleasantly tickled her sense of smell.

By way of goodbye, that night her mother gave her a long bath full of tender, silent little messages:

"Don't cry, Affi, good little girl. You were born with your soft skin, your brown skin, the color of ebony that the sun can't burn now, that thorns can't pierce now. You were born in the countryside, under the rain, after a violent storm. You're not afraid anymore, you mustn't cry now . . ."

Both of them were lying on the same big mat that Affi's grandmother had embroidered with palm leaves, one of them writhing, the other's outstretched tongue letting slip a string of viscous liquid accompanied by unbroken whispering, a maternal melody:

"Don't cry, Affi, good little girl, you were born with your soft skin, with your brown skin, the color of ebony that the sun can't burn now, that thorns can't pierce now, that the venom of even the deftest snakes can no longer penetrate. You were born in the countryside, under the rain, after a violent storm. You're not afraid, because life doesn't exist. You are empty. No one can give you a solid form. Cross, slide, surpass, overflow, cry and your tears will make you disappear into your own ocean."

THE GARBA BOUI-BOUI

The natural world exudes a striking beauty. The sun distills its dazzling rays on the village. Each leaf, each blade of grass receives its part, and worms and insects merrily warm themselves. The village streets rustle in the balmy wind that escorts rickshaws filled with merchandise. Men also exult in the gentle warmth, but those who have hard work to do or heavy loads to carry sigh under the hot caress of the tropical sun. The village follows the cadence of the sunlight, and everyone goes their own sweet way at their usual unhurried pace.

Sitting under a mango tree, Ada observes the daily scenes around her. Here, despair expresses itself only with silence; the greatest suffering is lived without a word. Here, human will is an illusion. Everyone knows that things are decided by custom. Individual choice? It doesn't exist. And Ada, who is sometimes on the brink of crisis, knows it well. Her life is a series of events decided by others. When the head of the family, tempted by the lure of a dowry, makes a decision, there's no going back. Dignity belongs primarily to the father, the family.

Ada is hungry, but no one offers her even a piece of dry manioc. She and her brothers are orphans, and they have to work nonstop to earn their daily bread. The entire village knows their lot in life, knows what it means for Ada and other children to be sitting under the mango tree.

So it is that around noon Ada takes her place at the foot of the tree to convey her hunger to the population. Her brothers are more reticent, but Ada sheds tears of despair. She seems to hold a grudge against the Fulani village: a place where no one sees anything, hears anything, or says anything. Ada is actually thinking back on all the troubles she encountered in her search for the Garba boui-boui, where Siliki's daughter Affi is confined. Although it causes her great sadness, she meditates on this adventure. She believes the villagers don't talk about it for fear of divulging secrets that would compromise many of them, including some of high rank.

◆◇◆

We finally found our way into the Garba boui-boui without help from anyone. To enter, you have to obtain permission from the caretaker. She opens the door for us. Ada, followed by her brothers and other people who have come a long way, enters somewhat apprehensively.

Initially, we glimpse a row of beds hidden behind partitions, which gives us the impression of being in a hospital.

Affi and her companions, having learned of the presence of strangers, withdraw to their beds. But the caretaker intercedes to reassure them. Though reserved, they come back one by one. There are five of them, and each stands in front of her bed. They are wearing just a piece of pagne around their waists, their bodies smeared with clay. They look healthy and don't appear to be suffering from their captivity.

Affi is barely twelve years old. Her father decided to marry her to Garba, the richest man in the village. Her four other companions in the boui-boui are about the same age.

Ada looks one of the young girls right in the eyes. Her face is refined with a flat little nose. Ada surrenders to the charm of this face wreathed in a halo of guilelessness now held captive to the boui-boui. Affi in turn seems to sense this feeling, this spontaneous inclination on Ada's part. Ada tells herself that she has to do something. She wants to talk to Affi, touch her. Their glances seek each other, cross, commune. In this young girl's eyes, Ada discovers a wide-open door, a whole world to explore. Affi, serene, seems to be the oldest of the bunch. Ada inevitably thinks back to Affi's mother. She had also heard the rumors. What was said in the village about the mother and daughter actually reassures her, though. Affi looks long and hard at Ada one more time before disappearing . . .

All Fulani women are shut up in obscurity for years like these girls; each has her own little area the size of her mat marked off by partitions. They have just enough room to stretch out or sit down. They are given meals and go outside for only a few minutes before dawn to wash. This is how these girls—ornamental gardens from families desperately overwhelmed by the acquisition of goods—are prepared for marriage.

In the distance stretches a succession of mountains and green hills. The road, a track wide enough for cars, is bordered by a quickset hedge made from stakes that have grown into real trees, bound together with reeds or bamboo.

I gaze for a long time at this landscape, so familiar and yet so unsettling. What does all of this mean in my overflowing imagination? Time erases everything. Time haunts me. I have the impression that time is running away with me. In my mind, everything is the present, and yet Siliki in this present is nothing but the past, and her appearance in the future requires and deserves the effort of reflection. This impression of absence is very strong. You feel it in the deepest part of you. Everything happens as if the present remained fixed, as if Siliki were resting her tender gaze on Ada, as if a lost bird had found its nest again, as if death were keeping so close to her that it was right there, present.

Troubled by the images rapidly passing before her eyes, Ada forces herself to reflect vigorously on this ritual. She asks a few trivial questions of the caretaker, who conceals the lines of sorrow on her face beneath a fearsome arrogance. Chewing kola, she speaks with her head held high: "Curiosity is a fine virtue, but it shouldn't be abused. Visits like this are rare and so precious that they require a special occasion or an exceptional request. Anthropologists and other researchers come sometimes, but this isn't a research center or a tourist site. This boui-boui comprises an integral part of our culture, like an institution that allows the village to function properly. The obscurity of the thing adds a certain charm that must be respected, in spite of oneself. Our boui-boui receives the pearls of the region, and visits like yours leave all sorts of traces: echoes, cries, and especially marks."

Abruptly, the caretaker grinds her teeth, spits out the kola remnants, and retorts sharply, "You're not the first or the last to pity the fate of these young girls. It's only a question of a man and his honor, maybe hard to understand, but should we seek to understand the absurd? My advice would be to disappear with these images. Your traces are easy to discern. Don't try anything in secret. It's useless to tell you things that are obvious. In the end, we always leave traces. A word to the wise."

At this, the caretaker closes the door so brusquely that the noise makes Ada jump from surprise and leaves goose bumps up and down her flesh. She stays there alone a moment without moving, rooted in place like a spent tree that refuses to fall, to leave the world of the forest. With a bitter taste in her mouth, the same as when sleepless nights of fleeting desires put you off too much drinking, Ada leaves the boui-boui compound, her heart weighted down with lead.

In her effacement, her invisibility, Affi's shadow still noticed the sad look on Ada's face. It is a shared sadness. Silence unites them, a silence that reaches the bottom of every chasm, the abyss of bitter anguish. Fear was fortifying their internal energies. Speech was emanating from silence. Doesn't muteness remain a useful form of resistance, even if it's humiliating? Some have the right to speak, others the right to silence. My life is only an interminable series of smothered cries, confounding my memories on dark and twisted paths. To overcome this vertigo would be to name it in all its unimaginable, yet somehow also imaginable, forms. Tirelessly, I cling to these cries in the hope that they

ıll pierce the imperceptible layer of the unsayable and slide
through the cracks. The silence that weighs in the deepest
part of a being remains a kind of dignity, the same dignity
that makes us quiver, that exiles us into our own sensations.
This discovery of strange sensations makes Affi so happy that
her heart smiles, for she never smiles externally, nor speaks,
nor expresses any physical sensation; everything is concentrated on the inside, in the hollow of inner emotions. Her
wound is a wound to the heart, and all wounds to the heart
are invisible. This happiness casts her into her mother's arms,
like in the past, casts her deep down into fervent nostalgia.
All kinds of sweet and tender images appear before her eyes.
The emotion is so great that Affi is unsure about what is real
and imaginary, a doubly painful moment. Peacefully, in slow
motion, Affi secretly wraps herself in these moments of pleasure in her mother's arms, a comfort for her survival. A bath.
A kiss. A story told to raise her morale. Despite all this, Affi
knows that her reality is located in the abyss of her village's
existence and that her mother is far away. She is nothing but
memories now.

From then on, in the reflection of a reflection, two women
waver in Affi's life, in her secret garden where fruits ripen
on the trunk of the tree of love. Her garden, always sunlit,
lets through a thread of golden light to shine onto beings
endowed with exceptional wisdom. Her mother gave her all
the most beautiful gifts in the world: secrets, that she will
share with another woman. Maybe this Ada, a stranger who
has infiltrated her heart, comes from her garden. Although
Affi doesn't know her, she is convinced that Ada is close,
despite her absence. Dreaming of this absolute desire, of the
fine fruit of passion for her future, seems as peculiar as all

this confinement. After these reveries, Affi lets a warm little tear slide down her cheek like a drop of ink that, maybe, will grow into a mark resembling a large scar, a sign of beauty but also of the sorrow that tradition makes you endure: a stamp of difference. The scar always emerges, even in the imagination. When it appears on the face, as visible as the rays of an encrusted emerald caught in an endless play of mirrors, the scar also bears the sign of an exemplary singularity. The scar's invisibility strikes painfully when it surfaces. Its characteristics explode every which way: it has a nasty taste; it reeks of all kinds of unpleasant aromas that make breathing difficult; it sounds a reveille that bursts the eardrums. No one doubts how much the sharpening of its knife knots the entrails and tears out the heart in grueling, endless pain. "The foot bitten by a snake always keeps the mark," as the wise old saying goes. The complexity of the glance that linked us also separated us. It frightened us. And so we looked at each other like two strangers lost in each other's arms, finding their way by a unique perfume: her mother's saliva, secret of friendship, sign of an impossible voyage.

The sun is shining down on figures perceptible under the mass of dust thrown up by the old cars congesting the roads. It's extremely hot, a burning heat, unbearable for the long walk that Ada is undertaking. She is sweating so much that her transparent pleated nylon skirt reveals all her intimate curves. Her panties, pink with black pinstripes, absorb so much sweat that the cotton stretches, letting her plump buttocks slip out. She wants to stop to wring out the panties. She's tired of having to keep raising her skirt to air out. How humiliating! But being alive simply means being humiliated. Living is a humiliation. She stops for a bit, lifts her skirt to dry her panties on a large stone she spies at the side of the road. She sits there with her legs open, and the rest of her body takes the opportunity to dry as well. Her whole pretty little forest is perspiring, and it's not at all disagreeable. With her panties dry, she can continue comfortably on her way.

◆◇◆

The first thing Ada looks at is the mountains in the distance, which she fixes with a stare full of reflection and her long struggle. Fear invades Ada. Until then, it had been an internal malaise, but she feels it transforming into violent sensations, rising up into her throat to the point where she wants to cry out, scream her anger, her humiliation. Let herself die so she won't suffer anymore, won't be subjected to humanity's foolishness anymore. Ah! How horrifying to suffer so much and not feel anything physically. Nostalgia and a great deal of sadness, a whole mix of emotions that she feels all at once. Ada has the impression that her body has left her, that the weight of her body has dragged her into infinity. Ada leaves the boui-boui's yard at a run, without waiting for her brothers or the other visitors who came from far-off countries. From the depths of forgetfulness, she awakes gracefully, like a snake long asleep in the shadows of anguish. She wants to flee the hell that she has just lived through. She must explore her limits quickly, break out of the nostalgic agony of events that sever the life of women. In the hazy slowness of events, she lets herself be cradled in the mist of the past, an effect of memory, which grows wane over time. Suddenly, she thinks back to the caretaker's words, and the word "trace" remains incrusted in her memory. Are they historical traces or simply traces that remain after every visit to the boui-boui?

Traces, traces, traces. The word contains a couple of sylla-bles. In fact, you can write traces and demonstrate that the letter "a" doesn't matter. It's in the middle of the word. You can pronounce the word "traces" quickly, emphasizing the first syllable, or put the stress on the last syllable, which whis-tles like a falling axe. Its pronunciation sounds the knell of history. These traces that the caretaker talked about must be able to set her on some useful tracks in this peaceful village, at once cruel and congenial, where the people are polite and very gentle. In this mystical atmosphere, it is pain that reigns, pain reflected in the salt-and-pepper hair of the elderly.

The silence reigning around here is frightening and trou-bles her own silence. There are only cars speeding by on the national road. Ada stays motionless for hours, and she is sur-prised to finally spy a shadow in the distance. A woman appears on the road, nude, muscular. Her arched body recalls the form of a classical guitar. Her gait is supple and grace-ful. A basket of sweet potatoes is poised on her head, surely her day's food that she is bringing back from the field; axe, machete, and scraper rest on top of the sweet potatoes. At Ada's approach, she quickly scales the ladder of the hedge and disappears. One more of these women who erases her-self from her own existence. Worse than the crayfish that slip through your fingers, this woman evaporates before Ada's eyes. She was just able to make out the silhouette of her breasts, pointed like needles. Ada's hand rises to bid a sad adieu.

◆◇◆

Ada raises her eyes to the immense, bluish sky, grimacing from the blinding rays of the sun at its zenith which floods everything with dazzling, uniform light. Magnificent country, where life is intense and mysterious. It is also a hard life lived by these Fulani, the ones from the mountain, a derisive name used by neighboring villages. A population who cultivates earth that is too dense, who must struggle against nature to live. Thin bodies, waists girded with a meager, tattered pagne, torsos covered with sweat, often a leg disfigured from a wound that went untended or healed poorly. They walk quickly, knees bent slightly like porters whose burden is too heavy. They bear baskets on their heads, some filled with poultry, sweet potatoes, yams, others with various gourds of oil and palm wine. Where are these men going? And these naked women, with their firm, well-rounded buttocks that they shake beneath of bit of pagne, walking at a pace slowed to the rhythm of the tam-tam drums on the sunlit paths. Women, Ada is looking for you. Women, where are you? Come out to meet Ada who loves to watch you slowly sway to the rhythm of inaudible music to which only the body gives meaning. What Ada loves even more is the emotion she experiences when one of these women appears on her path.

Exhausted by her reflections, Ada loses all sense of time and space. The night cradles her in her misfortune, and she doesn't even wake to hear the storm rumbling. When she comes round the next morning, fatigue and discouragement interlace in her desperate heart. But everything around her seems grand and beautiful. The sky is lovely and luminous. For the superstitious, a day of predilection. The storm had swooped down on the Fulani village, and water swept the streets, flooded courtyards, like a big spring cleaning. The thunder rumbled and lightning rent the sky while frightened children huddled in the farthest corner of their huts. The temperature dropped ten degrees during the night. It hadn't rained for two years. Day then broke on a new note as clouds raced across a fiery horizon. The village awakens feverish, garrulous. The countryside seems to be emerging from a long, sweet state of lethargy.

The clemency of the heavens has given the signal for renewed activity, and each person is conscious that something essential has just happened which it would be futile to ignore. The atmosphere is full of elation: sweat drips from faces; laughter and cries echo in the plain; the women, with their swaying gait, bring refreshments and words of comfort to the men who wipe clean the paths and entrances to the huts cluttered with debris. At nightfall, stiff, exhausted, but happy with their accomplished duty, they fall asleep instantly. This great burst of solidarity uniting peasant men and women is a symbol of the peace in their souls. Ada thinks of her own mother and grandmother. She wonders if they knew this mountain atmosphere where the slow pace of life gives the soul repose. How heavy life is in these mountains!

ADA AND SILIKI

The fairies of Ada's memory begin to haunt her like flames consuming a virgin forest. She observes the village and its inhabitants in detail: life is peaceful there, yet the atmosphere frightens her. She wants to catch hold of the village's destiny with all her might. Some force, however, prevents her from doing so. And at that moment, the awful cruelty of her life becomes evident. Blow for blow, and faced with the reappearance of so many deftly dissimulated sorrows, how can she not turn toward the mirror of her own thought? Ada goes back through her life, hunting through her memories, the reasons for her suffering, advancing blindly into a whirlwind of ashes.

Orphaned from her mother, Ada grew up with her brothers and other children in the large courtyard that occupies nearly the entire entrance to the village. She doesn't really know her father, since every male of a certain age is called Baba. The village antennas often announce bits of disjointed information to her about her biological Baba: he was basically a man exasperated by all his wives and children. Without really knowing her mother's story, the villagers take pleasure in defiling her name. No one knows the true story of Ada's mother, except for Siliki, the old legless witch who lives in a hut beside the backwater pool. The space she inhabits feeds the mystery surrounding her person, her hut, and the pool. Every season, someone disappears into the pool, and each disappearance represents a new tale that enters the repertoire of legends—another useful lesson for all the generations to come in her father's village. Ada doesn't consider him to be her real Baba. She feels like a stranger to that whole story. It's only by chance that she's the daughter of that particular Baba. Unfortunately, accidents of birth are just part of the human condition.

◆◆◆◆

The story of Siliki's life is told and retold, each time taking on new moments of suspense, new entertaining turns, stirring and terrifying. The more she hears about this woman, the more Ada's passion for her grows, provoking one sole desire: to gain admittance to her refuge. Her disgusting body attracts her like a flower attracts a bee. Her squalid story also piques Ada's interest; she feels passionately about the so-called anomaly of this woman. The world of the unnamable holds great attraction for her. She feels peculiar and out of place in her Baba's household. What the others find bad, Ada finds good; those are precisely the things she's most passionate about. For example, loving their fellow people disgusts everyone around her. It's simply unbearable to them.

◆◇◆

A sharp pain grips my throat every time the circle gathers around the fire to delight once more in telling stories about Siliki. That creature represents the abject: a legless body. Ada tries so hard to be deaf in one ear that she's now in the habit of only hearing the other speak. In the village, stories about Siliki are repeated in every form, and each night, new elements as yet unknown must be added. With Siliki stories, the young people in the village learn how to become good orators. They measure themselves against each other. The person who succeeds in eliciting the most laughter receives praise for days afterward. Siliki truly captures the village's imagination.

One evening, Ada hears herself cry out like a wild beast, a sign that her disgust has attained its perfection; it is the moment when one loses oneself in rage and its abyss. That day, Ada decides to give her own version of the story of the old legless witch. No matter what, she must tell her own story, which includes the stories of all women without voices, condemned to muteness. Among the Fulani, women always listen to stories about other women without contesting them. The stories about the old witch Siliki are known to all of them, but no woman dares give her version of it. For Ada, the possibility of losing herself in humiliation flies away under a cloud of unhappy thoughts. Now she has access only to melancholy and the beauty of sunlit days. The disability that she has long brooded over sees her absurdity in extremis. But the fear in her heart is great, for the Siliki myth has predictable effects on the village and its inhabitants. No one ventures alone around the private domain of the one whom everyone in the village rejects because of her disability her stench, her witchcraft, her solitude.

The women in her Baba's household don't feed Ada unless she works for hours on end, and when she refuses to, she wastes away with hunger. Sometimes she eats so many green mangoes with salt that she gets a stomach ache. One day, she is exhausted by the heat and the long hours of tedious household chores, but the cries of a crowd from the village square still attract her attention. People are running from every direction, panic-stricken mothers search for their children, fearful men mutter threatening words. The luminous ghost has ventured into the village at last—the witch has come out of her abyss. The feeling of uneasiness that Ada experiences in Siliki's presence paralyzes her legs. Then the panic of the moment thrusts her into Siliki's arms. The two of them are carried by her weight, and their bodies topple over with a heavy thud that attracts an astonished and fearful crowd whose curiosity nonetheless incites pleasure in this meticulous exhibition of taboo: the legless witch fastened like a larva to the body of the one nobody dares name, that base child. She is just as vile as the witch. To signal their anger, the villagers call her all sorts of names other than the one her mother gave her, the name she loves so much: Ada. Fortunately her brothers are there to remember it. Ada, handicapped from birth by her mother's reputation, bears the label of sin that her sweet mother committed among the Mafa, those pitiless ancestors. The Mafa, a mountain people with traditions that must absolutely not be questioned, respect ancestral law to the letter. That's how today, at this precise moment, the word Mafa crosses Ada's lips.

The curious scene and everything that has led up to it nurtures hate, disgust, and malediction. The village assembles into a motionless crowd. Should this event be celebrated or lamented? Confusion reigns. Ada is disgust incarnate, just like Siliki. It is ultimately fear that reigns in the hearts of the villagers. Angry, ill at ease, the crowd lets loose as one. They are finally tasting the pleasure of this long-awaited spectacle. Scandal is offered up to them like free wine. All of them had been waiting for the day when the cursed Ada would disappear, and that day has finally come. In any case, since the question of marriage had automatically been excluded from the list of possibilities offered Ada by the human condition, she feels herself slipping away. Like vapor vanishing into the distance, she decides to flee. The whole village is there, but she wishes that they, too, would disappear into their sad little huts that the sun never brightens. Ada refuses to share this act with them. She wants to undertake it alone.

Ada has never seen a person without legs. Siliki, whose torso is covered with fat, is crushing Ada's little body lost under the heap of her rags. Despite the weight of Siliki's bust, Ada feels good wrapped in the arms of the unknown woman. The cries and insults from the villagers reach her under a fresh melody of fragrant, floral spring. The revolting smell of Siliki's rags makes Ada nauseous, and she vomits. All the green mangoes that her stomach has so much trouble digesting come back up. Vomiting delivers Ada from the pain of stomach cramps that her gluttony so often inflicts on her, though she needs to nourish herself with whatever food she can find. Softly, to console herself for her jumbled emotions, she begins to cry. The worst is the heat. Suddenly, a piece of cloth brushes against my mouth where the remaining vomit struggles to emerge. What gentleness! What sensitivity! Siliki's hairy arms enclose Ada's frail little body in a brusque movement that lifts Siliki onto her shoulders. Now the cries are joined with pebbles and other dangerous objects that Siliki receives on her back and head. Under the brutal shocks arriving from every direction, Siliki signals Ada to go faster by tapping her a few times on the head. Siliki envelops Ada in her stinking rags, but Ada is happy because no one has ever taken care of her. Her brothers are there for her, but it's not the same. This time it's a woman offering Ada her embrace and gentleness. Ada has the impression that she's committing the wildest act of her existence that day. Her view is blocked by Siliki's rags, but she can hear loud cries expressing scandal, fear, scorn, and flight. Her nudity repulses the crowd; a sort of common guilt imposes itself at the sight of her disability. A tear slides onto Ada's cheek. Normally, Siliki drags herself around at a turtle's pace, but this time it is Ada who advances slowly. Siliki's body on her shoulders forms the turtle's shell, and Ada feels herself embodying that animal.

Ada and Siliki cross the village like one of those terrible cyclones that leaves only ruins behind; the strength of the collective seems to have collapsed under Siliki's presence. The silence that imposes itself as they pass is a silence that speaks volumes. The discomfort the village experiences when faced with Siliki's body is contagious. It penetrates their own bodies from top to toe with a feeling of resigned powerlessness. Like Siliki and Ada, they are all handicapped somehow; their bodies are abject, too, even if they don't know it. The physical evidence of Siliki's disability is an obvious fact. But for all the villagers present, there's a different kind of handicap: powerlessness in the face of the events that govern their lives. In any case, Ada suffers from the same handicap—silence. Starting with language itself, which is completely hostile to Ada. Often when she wants to speak, the words don't come out. Ada's handicap is expressed by the powerlessness of not being able to communicate her deepest thoughts, improbability before the word of the moment, and anguish at her own doubt. Relationships with others can be represented by a bank account with debits and credits—the balance is never stable. In the village, people are sure of themselves. They make others suffer without realizing the harm they've caused, and so the courtyard of Ada's Baba is a place of great pain. The terminology of the word handicap in that courtyard is defined by the villagers' refusal when faced with their own selves and the elements that make up their lives. The women in Ada's Baba's yard know how to play. They swiftly shed their handicap by projecting it onto another. Ada is their whipping girl. Despite all that, Ada knows deep down that the whole village is nothing but creatures who are abject, base, sullied by life itself. Ada thinks of these women and smiles from within the intimacy of her sorrow. Now she is far from all that. She is nothing but smoke. How poignant! Ada withdraws from the village with Siliki on her shoulders.

◆◇◆

Ada is astonished to encounter the calm of a private space, but ironically, the absence of so many people calls to mind her Baba's courtyard again. She has often dreamed of these moments of peace—inaccessible moments, but so present in her future condition. Once Siliki is seated on the skin of a leopard that, according to her, had devoured many animals, she thanks Ada and says, "The road is short that unites friends." Her sensitivity, gentleness, and extreme courtesy are all remarkable, but for the people in the village, she remains the madwoman, the legless witch with the suffocating smell. Siliki's physical appearance is frankly repugnant, but fortunately she is kind, and every day with her is a day of joy, of rediscovered hope. The speed at which their relationship transforms itself doesn't worry Ada at all. Not only is she used to the cries of children, but also to the cries of adults frustrated for so long by daily life. The village is noisy, but no one really speaks to anyone else; rather, they scream in protest. Calm only comes at night when the village is asleep. But the depths of night signify another drama in the courtyard of Ada's Baba. There's a semblance of peace when her Baba isn't there, but the nights he spends with the cleaning woman are often accompanied by long cries ascending into the silence.

With Siliki, silence signifies the grandeur of her spirit. Speech is limited at our home, but our moments of communication are deeply intense. The voice commits an act of aggression that transforms Siliki into an old leaf—shriveled, clammy, rotten. Ada wants to discover the real Siliki, but she is elusive. To get to know this woman, Ada tells herself, virtually all the barriers must be broken. Siliki fulfills her. She knows how to make Ada laugh, which is rare. She is a sad, silent person; only the look in her eyes conveys her pain. Siliki understands how to make her forget her dread on damp mornings. Ada wants to talk all the time, to pose questions. She seems agitated, scattered in every direction, but it's all because of how good she feels. Knowing the other is an incredibly difficult experience, even when communication comes easily. But with muteness, it's even worse; it's a giant puzzle in pieces that you have to put back together while an impatient child pesters you. The silence around Siliki's refuge envelops Ada in utter melancholy. The enigma of her difficult and irresolute existence has transformed her into a melancholy person, but her melancholy actually frees her from all anguish and floats in a bubble of purple flowers. Ada feels good at this woman's side, this Siliki, the legless witch. She soars through the transports of pleasure. And so does Siliki.

With the silence that dominates the surroundings, it's possible to distinguish the different voices in the chatter of the forest: between the songs of the birds and local insects, between the cries of beasts and the sound of the wind making the leaves sing. Siliki asks me to listen: "Ada, listen to the hissing serpent. It's pretty, isn't it?" Curled up in her pain, Ada holds onto a bit of hope. Hope rebounds at certain moments, like short-circuits on stormy nights when lightning slashes the sky and startles eyes that had been furtively cast outdoors. But for Ada, it's impossible to feel happy for very long; happiness invades her suddenly and then disappears as swiftly as a lightning bolt.

She often thinks of her two brothers and the village. Maybe her brothers, who protected her from Baba's malicious wives, will come to see her face. No, they won't be sinking into sadness over this; they often encouraged her to run away. She wonders if they're glad, in the end, about her flight. Perhaps they sense the safety that Siliki's refuge offers her. One thing is certain: no one will come near here. Siliki's refuge is a mystery. Ada's brothers must simply be glad that she has finally succeeded in leaving that foul space. Her Baba's household is a cursed place. Whatever their thoughts, Ada knows in her heart that they are and always will be with her. Her brothers are prisoners of her Baba, who is the master of his courtyard in which he transforms everyone into slaves. Everyone works for him and his fields. His cocoa business makes him everyone's master. Like every other master in this world, Ada's Baba is often away, traveling in various countries. Days pass without anyone in the courtyard calling for Ada. The village forgets her so quickly—how strange! The idea of being an exile without a family enchants her; then her nomadism will represent a choice, the choice her brothers always wished for her. Ada imagines how much her brothers must have suffered from always hearing nasty words gushing from mouths thirsty for slander, even if something—good or bad—must be said to mark the present event. The collective shame of rumor no longer exists for her, since the entire village had not pardoned the sin committed by the mother she never even knew. From the rumors, Ada only understands that her poor mother was cursed. Impossibility. Interdiction. The idea of fleeing this courtyard had nagged ardently at Ada for a long time. It's hardly possible to suffer like that. The fierce feeling of powerlessness, of inexpressibility is terrible. Ada curls up in her pain.

◆◇◆◇◆

Smiling, Siliki holds out her hand. "Come," she says to me. "Let's go for a walk around the pool." Sitting on a rock, Siliki and Ada look at the water in the still, yellowish pool. They stay that way a long time, not tiring either of the view or the position of their bodies. A light wind blows, delicately caressing the foliage around them. Unable to imagine the power of silence by herself, Ada places her hand on Siliki's; she wants to feel her skin on hers. Siliki talks to her so gently. Her voice is cracked, thin, and reedy, purer than that of the hissing serpent she loves to listen to. She explains to Ada that the hissing serpent has a sharp cry that delicately pierces one's hearing. The sound of the snake strokes the eardrum pleasurably, allowing it to detect the depth of sounds mingled together in the forest. Often or almost always, the cries of animals who have disappeared alone into the night are muffled by Siliki and Ada's incessant chatter. There are moments when they talk too much, in spite of the silence that fills the other moments of their daily existence. Silent, Ada listens without interrupting Siliki. With her two hands, she caresses Siliki's, delicately massaging them, and in return Siliki repeats the same gestures while a teardrop slides between their fingers. Siliki kindly tells her not to cry anymore. Her tenderness covers Ada's face with tears of joy. She turns around without moving her hands and licks Ada's face several times. Ada wriggles with pleasure as the sensation of the tongue on her check fills her heart with rare happiness. The reflection of the countryside sinks into the rays of a gleaming sun.

They are perspiring big drops of sweat, since the heat is beating down on them, as it does every early afternoon. Siliki undresses and drags her body to the backwater. She disappears under the water for a few seconds. Ada watches her body writhe like a fish, then Siliki smiles at Ada and holds her arm out to her while the other arm maintains the balance of her body in the water. Without legs, she swims only with her arms. Ada is afraid of the water: she is afraid of this pool in particular, and she doesn't even know how to swim. She doesn't want to go into the water of this mysterious pool. She feels good where she is, sitting on the rock. Plus, she hasn't forgotten the legends about the backwater where generations of villagers have disappeared. As she thinks back on these stories once again, her life spent in the village flies rapidly by in front of her like when someone is drowning. Oh! It's awful to admit, but Ada is awfully afraid of the backwater. If only she could change into a little goldfish, she wouldn't hesitate an instant to disappear into the water with Siliki. She is far off in her thoughts when she hears Siliki's voice. Her arm is still waiting for Ada's. "Come," she says, "the water is nice. Come on, I'm here. Don't be afraid." Ada smiles in turn while she makes a sign of refusal with her head. She has the impression of having refused something of herself, but she cannot risk herself in the pool. With a harsh grinding of teeth, Siliki disappears into the depths of the water, is lost for a moment. The water evokes perfect harmony in her life.

The wild flowers shine in the glare of the sun like in a man-made garden. Illuminated suddenly by the inspiration of the moment, Ada combines the colors of the flowers into a bouquet. She hides it behind the rock and waits for Siliki to hold her hand out to her again to slip the bouquet between her fingers. Siliki swims a long time, enjoying herself with the fish and the other inhabitants of the pool. She loves the water, particularly the water of this pool. She admires it for its wildness—blessed with natural charm—and for all her friends, the beasts and plants, that linger there. When Siliki comes out of the water, Ada sees that her chest is remarkably beautiful, and the impossible overcomes her; she desires Siliki with all her might. Her body opens and burns with the flames of desire.

In a confused mixture of joy and distress, Siliki places an unbridled kiss on Ada's forehead. She feels the tension of her breathing. Ada stays seated next to Siliki for a long time. They don't speak to each other. Only their breathing and the sounds of their bodies emerge from the silence. Around their refuge, the noises of the forest superimpose themselves over the silence.

In a gesture full of tenderness, Siliki takes Ada's hand and says, "Since the weather is so beautiful today, I'll tell you the story of my life." Ada sits up straight as if to prepare to listen. Everything in their refuge seems calm, except for the songs of birds and other animal cries that break the rhythm of the silence. Siliki speaks slowly.

"It came as a big surprise when my father threw a large pagne over my head and took me to a secluded hut at the edge of the Fulani village. When I was shut up in that hut, I missed my mother terribly, but I tried to take my troubles patiently. The caretaker liked me a lot and always favored me. She paid me a compliment: she thought I had a pretty smile. A smile, she said, that she liked to admire. She often tried to entertain me, sometimes by telling stories where she would laugh all by herself, sometimes by bringing me good fruit from her house and games to kill the time. She bored me immensely, so I offered her some reflections on her good acts. Entertainment is an excellent idea, but in savoring it, why shouldn't we do so in a useful and worthy manner, I mean, in working for the well-being of others? Everyone, according to their talents and situation, can act toward this noble goal instead of wasting—killing—time by seeking to divert themselves. The very word "divert" is revealing in the context: its etymology, *devertere* in Latin, means to turn away from an aim. It's the opposite of *con*version. Diversion means leaving the path one should follow to commit to an entirely different route. The distractions to which the caretaker wanted to lead me served absolutely no purpose, for my route was already traced. Nothing could conduct me away from it, certainly not a few distractions. When she saw that these forms of entertainment didn't suit me, the caretaker left me in peace until my marriage. I had known during this time how to keep my mind intact and alert so that nothing could make me give in to misery. Even if I were dressed in rags, cold, or hungry, it didn't matter—as long as I could read, think, and observe the plants, I felt free spiritually."

◆◇◆

"Sorrow plunged my poor mother into that long, lonely sleep of no return. I learned the news the day of my marriage, since everyone was there except her. I roamed through the crowd looking for the glance of a close acquaintance, a friend of my mother's named Tàata. My mother came from a far-off land. She had for friend, sister, neighbor, this Tàata, a very kind woman. If Mama was not there, Tàata would be, there was no doubt. According to tradition, Tàata shouldn't normally take part in the ceremony, which concerned only the close family of the husband and wife. Tàata shouldn't have been there at all, in principle. It made my heart bleed to see her eyes rimmed with fatigue and distress, her voice trembling at the end of sentences from the sobs nearly strangling her, the traces of protruding nerves, and the sweat mixed with tears on her face. In a familiar embrace, Tàata took me in her arms and whispered something faintly into my ear as she slipped me a packet of papers wrapped in a piece of pagne: 'It's the wedding gift your mama wanted you to receive.' She squeezed my hand and then disappeared into the crowd. From that moment on, my body became subject to a painful desire for hatred. The upheaval dragged me into a long meditation that turned me into a vegetable.

"At night, my body didn't react at all. With my teeth clenched all night long, I would relive the sweet moments of my childhood: the backwater pools, little quarrels between friends, the fire and the stories Mama told, warm pancakes—all the family atmosphere with Mama. A light smile passed across my lips when I would think back on the neighbor's mangy dog. That dog was unbelievable. When he sat down somewhere, he'd have a whole colony of flies on his ears.

Everyone used to beat him because he was responsible for stealing all the missing meat and fish left to dry next to kitchens. From time to time, blinded by desire, he would chase down a she-dog until they reached the sexual act which ended with loud cries of pain, not to mention how the poor she-dog had strayed to be trapped by the dog's sex—animal instinct, surely. The she-dog's last sigh of joy and pleasure would always come at the moment of brutal penetration, followed by the last sigh of calm when the dog extracted himself. We really liked that mangy dog, in spite of his disgusting sores.

"Lost in sadness on that first unforgettable night when my husband raped me all night long as he repeated the gesture of penetration like an animal, I was reminded of what that mangy dog used to do to all the she-dogs that crossed his path. But no cry escaped into that night where all the village gossips waited impatiently for dawn before the door to the nuptial chamber. It's unbelievable, but the pain of others gave those frigid old spies pleasure. Juicy gossip was limited, and no one could believe this drama: the defeat that my husband had just suffered. The tittle-tattle about it was uttered in a series of rather banal sentences: we have the proof of her virginity, but the sound effects weren't there like with every other young woman. The music of bodies was muffled in the silence of that night veiled by violence. The absence of crude moans represents a failure of the man's virility. Not only must my virginity be proven but I also have to scream like a cow, even if I don't feel anything—those are the rules of the game. All the other women respect the ritual without fail. But the wheel no longer turned at the same cadence; memory no longer reproduced its age-old tale."

The swollen waters roared through the bed of the little river encumbered by rocks. Huge trees tried vainly to catch up with their branches caught in the muddy cascades, while lianas trailed in the water like little black snakes. From between the giant roots that plunged into the water there emerged from time to time the glinting muzzle of a crocodile who partook in listening to Siliki's tale.

"You see, you're welcome here. All my friends are signaling their friendship. Listen carefully."

The force of Siliki's voice awakens her entire realm, not because she speaks loudly but because her voice overflows with a strength that envelops every creature's soul in immense joy. As soon as the animals hear the sound of her voice, they settle down, become attentive. All the beasts are present as if it were a family meeting. The closest animals surround the rock we're sitting on and, from time to time, little piercing cries of joy erupt spontaneously as a sign of solidarity, to assure Siliki that her audience is awake and listening.

Siliki catches her breath. "What a beautiful wedding gift Tàata gave me!" she tells me in a whisper. "Some beings have such a strong sensibility, I thought to myself, when I finally unwrapped the packet of letters left by Mama. Was it Mama who had asked that they be given to me? Still more questions, nothing but questions trotting through my mind. I didn't need to convince myself of Mama's love. I sang her praises in my head. I talked only to myself because there was no one else to tell about that formidable woman. I lived in a mystery that only shadows could illuminate. Blinded by the anger that ruled my existence, I waited days before discovering what my mother had written. I wanted to be alone to read her messages. At the end of a narrow path that follows the riverbank then climbs the slope and snakes across roots and blocks of granite, there was a poor, forsaken hut. I slipped into a corner of it with my little kerosene lamp, not paying any attention to the occupants. Once comfortably settled and with my eyes closed, I first took the packet of letters between my hands and held them tightly against me before bringing them to my nose to see if I could recognize Mama's scent. My mother wrote on whatever she found lying about. There were signs inscribed on tree roots and banana leaves, on newspapers and scraps of paper. The ink had disappeared in places from the roots and leaves. Some of her signs and even the writing remained indecipherable. There were gaps in the text, words whose ink had vanished. From time to time, I encountered blank spaces that were an integral part of the writing. Key words, verbs were missing from their precise places. In short, comprehension proved impossible. But despite all these difficulties, I didn't lose hope. It was only a question of time or space for me. Faced with that immense, tedious task, my eyes grew tired as they crossed the dull pages which evoked so little at first sight. Nothing is easily accessible, Ada, especially not knowledge, the knowledge that I wished to attain. It is only in the intranquility of the soul that one finds tranquility. Every day, I applied myself to reading, like a child who has discovered a forbidden book. I repeated the same gestures on humid nights weighted down by thick layers of heavy mist. Once I had arrived at my secret abode, I would take the packet of letters, leaves, and bits of root from between my thighs, clasp them to my chest, and then hold them up to my nose to pleasure in the odors of old things. I would carefully remove the string from the documents that were so precious to me. Without despair, indifferent to the raging wind outside, I would pose my eye upon the writing and try to make out a few words, sentences, paragraphs. Finally one day, a messenger came to alert my husband about my nocturnal activities, and I was no longer able to retreat to the hut to try to decipher Mama's writing. Yet one more pleasure that my husband and the others took from me without remorse. Cruelty is part of our customs. At this point in my life, each painful image that passes before my eyes remains as striking as all the other images incrusted in my memory over time. I'm not well, and my wounds are bleeding anew, like the blood that flows when the executioner strikes the condemned in one swift blow."

◆◆◆◆

"After a relatively calm pregnancy, the moment of delivery came, followed by a tradition that I had to respect in my turn, like all my husband's other wives. I was ready to execute the full performance. An old woman was sent who attended all my husband's wives during their deliveries. Her name was Mánna. I don't remember all the details very well, but as soon as old Mánna caught the baby, she sprayed it with water from her mouth to make the baby cry, allowing it to expel any salty water that might still be in its nose. If the saltwater stayed in the nose, the baby would have an unpleasant smell for the rest of its life and talk through its nose, she told me. Everything went very well. I had a daughter in my arms. I smiled at her. She was warm, and her heat warmed my heart. I looked at her for a long time with the tender eyes of a happy mother. I named my daughter Affi, the pearl around my neck. Affi: that child was a real pearl.

Her presence caused my secret to re-emerge, the secret that I had kept buried in the bottom of my heart. I had to repress it, always repress it, and live only in my imagination. And then from that point on: hatred. I lived in hate, and my daughter would carry the same words seasoned with hatred, the venom that pricks and poisons the blood of all oppressed people: rage!

"With the passage of time, the village grew accustomed to my calm. Everything seemed to return to order. And so, with my daughter, I decided to take back up the decipher-ing of my mother's writing. I sensed that my mother had transmitted something to me whose secret I should have pen-etrated. I quickly rediscovered my passion for the work. I was nearly obsessed by the research. I sacrificed myself to get there. Mama had told me one day, when I was little: you will work very hard to get something; in our culture, nothing is inherited, everything is conquered.

"Like all the other women, I possessed my little hut with my child, and our husband came to visit once a week to relieve himself sexually. You simply had to wait in your hut for your turn at fornication. That word makes me nauseous, but what other word is there to use? It's the only one that crosses my enraged lips. When a baby was born, the other women would take care of the washing and cooking for a year, just enough time for the baby to acquire more auton-omy. I shut myself up in my hut with my daughter and plunged back into ceaseless reading. Nothing but her little cry of hunger could extract me from my reading and scrib-bling. To play the role assigned to me, however, I would go out draped in pagnes and take the little one for walks to get some sun.

"Relentlessly, I set to work every day. The sun would set without me even noticing that the noxious damp and darkness were signaling the presence of a night that would be long. Whenever I had the impression that I had reconstructed a text, I would find other bits of paper and notes scratched on roots. From all that jumble of writing—that superb prose where the rhythm of the sentence enveloped me—I succeeded, bit by bit, in weaving a tapestry of my mother's words."

Why me. Why me. I beg for forgiveness. Forgiveness!

Man, I detest you and you are going to die. You will die with the same suffering you inflicted upon me . . . See my body, murmurs the right leg, it is red, red with the blood of a man from some other place, a land where it snows. He attacked me. Hey! Man, you are going to die and you'll see pain before you succumb. Hey! Man. Look at my other leg, growls the left leg, it is gashed open. Why did you want my marrow? And what did you want to do with my body? Hey! Man! my mouth cries out as it laughs loudly. I ask for pity. Pity. Pity. Woman, save my soul. Woman, do you hear me? Save me, woman! Why don't you help me? I was bad to you, yes, but will you forgive me? Help me, woman. I loved you, woman. Woman!

So a snigger suppressed the cries of pain in my throat. And I saw, I saw him, him, the solitary one, the giant, the chevalier of my nights . . . Your big arms thrash about and . . . help! He hits my flanks, he opens them with hatchets, machetes! His spiteful gaze suffocates me, strangles me . . . Woman! My blood is spurting, your body is turning red now . . . Man, you carry the inscription of my pain upon you. I am suffering, my pain is intense. An infernal circle of horrible hairy dwarves, their long arms hanging down, dance around me. Their circle closes, they keep turning, so quickly that I only see a black circle around me, squeezing me, squeezing me . . .

Man, I know you'll come back. You've been prowling around me for ten years.

Meanwhile I race across the world, I flee from men, but they still prowl around me. Man, you hound me. I continue to ask the woman for forgiveness, I beg her to help me. Woman! It's always a mistake to try to prove existence through reason instead of going to see and touch the actual thing. Woman, I ask your forgiveness. Woman!

They're kind to me here. They gave me a little room, nicely closed, nicely padded, that they keep locked . . . what does it matter! Those men will come back even so . . . I know it . . . They're spying on me . . . even here . . . That's how the intern, you know, the big red one . . . with the big arms, well, I'll tell you . . . he's my husband . . . Do you understand? Don't say a word about it. Ah! but I'll defend myself . . . See this knife . . . and this rope . . . I stole them from him yesterday . . . at the bougossi . . . and when he comes, I'll tie this rope to his ridgepole; with my knife, I'll sever his roots, then, with my mouth, I'll delve into his heart to take back my blood. I'll suck him eagerly.

These pages were torn from the tense hands of a madwoman who, they say, lost her reason after the disappearance of her child whom she had come to find in the Fulani village.

Ada listens passionately. She doesn't understand everything Siliki tells her. But what is essential in the story doesn't escape her, although the details are sometimes too personal. In the dark, with just a narrow slice of light, Siliki often scribbles on anything she can lay her hands on. She spends hours bent over, her fingers lost in a burst of writing. Knowing Siliki, she accomplishes everything that her heart dictates her to do, but Ada can't manage to grasp the meaning of all her gestures. With quotation marks, one opens and closes the parenthesis as one likes. It's possible to modify, to add, to fill the void; quotation marks, at least, allow for infiltration at any moment. One weaves one's existence with the intentions of others, all the while leaving gaps, for some threads of reflection are elusive, despite a degree of mastery acquired from weaving one's thoughts methodically. All this generates excitement, of course. More and more, Ada delves into her curiosity for this stranger who has since become none other than her very dearly beloved, her sweet Siliki. Her surprise increases after the reading of Siliki's mother's text. The ambiguity of the enigma doesn't interrupt the process as a whole.

Ada has the impression that she knows the heart of the secret, the layer of shadows that make up the story of Siliki's mother, but that doesn't disperse the shadows in her own mind. Ada thinks about what people say in her Baba's yard: "like mother, like daughter." But is that the case in this story, the one about Siliki and her mother? Ada dreams of discovering the whole story, the story of Siliki herself. She understands that from now on, time is precious. Little by little, she cultivates her friendship with her beloved, who reveals all the secrets of life, the ones that transform shadows into slivers of light. As long as their friendship lasts, she'll horsewhip the passing time, allowing her to be done with sorrows while she's far from her Baba's yard. Her story, that is, Siliki's, is a story that Ada is not ashamed to permit into her dreams, even if it must enter through the tiny door of the smallest detail that incrusts itself onto her memory forever. And so it isn't at all necessary to recount her distress in detail. Ada suffers as much from the void as from not knowing anything about Siliki's life, and she often ends up choked by her sobs.

How did she become disabled and where is her daughter Affi? The more Ada's curiosity spills over, the more mysterious Siliki becomes. The layer of mystery that covers her shadow requires her to remain hardened. Siliki tells Ada stories, but not about herself. Ada thinks about all the stories Siliki tells her under their pillow, and she smiles as she recalls an old legend about the village of Siliki's husband. She knows every little detail about this legend. She smiles a long time. But alas! It's still just an old legend that doesn't add anything to the knowledge that interests her most. An opening into Siliki's life must be found as soon as possible, even if it's nothing more than a fissure, a sliver of light that will finally brighten the shadows where Ada lives her life with the woman she loves. The illumination of the opening, the fissure, projects the beginnings of hope and displaces the traces of despair. Ada can already weave a tale with the trivial information Siliki has divulged to her. But what about her daughter? Where is she now? That troubles Ada. And her husband, the Fulani village? How sad! Ada veers from impasse to impasse; all she has are questions that expand the mystery that is Siliki. Curled up around herself, Ada remains shaken by all the emotions that beset her over the long days, the architecture of time. Siliki surely knows the story of Ada's mother because they are both Fulani. Ada's Baba had left the Fulani village like Siliki to settle with the Mafa. After having received so many strangers who ended up staying on, the Mafa village was formed by people from elsewhere, people without traces, without roots. Now the Mafa themselves comprise a large population of old people who surely came from elsewhere, too, but adapted to the environment and traditions they maintain.

✦◇✦◇✦

When Siliki shares her mother's story, Ada can sense in her gaze how sadness invades her day after day. Ada's love for Siliki keeps growing. She feels so good with her; Siliki has become the source of her happiness. She is so in love with Siliki and she offers her flowers and little kisses whenever the opportunity presents itself. Ada's heart is in bloom with love: her mouth, her modest hands, a ballet of inborn shadows . . . Ada dreams, dreams, loses herself in the happiness of the moment.

Like an attacking ant, Ada, who has decided to cultivate Siliki's heart still further, comes up against the impossible. Siliki, much older than Ada, understands that life demands more than their love, more than their happiness. Life as a pair doesn't completely conceal the serious wounds scarred onto their souls. Their stories are engraved on a nest of sorrows. The hatred that crisscrosses these stories has marked only too well the reality of other women. Ada wants to understand the story of her own mother, but she takes time to reflect. How can she pose questions to Siliki? A question asked here and there will open the source of pain. And so they each decide internally to imagine beautiful tales, demanding and courageous tales to make up for lost time, to provide comfort. Curiously, they understand each other in a sort of mute proclamation. Ada whispers, alone, for only herself to hear, but Siliki is still included there, like a flower emerging from a plant that was taken from nature and transferred somewhere else, just for one's own pleasure.

This Siliki is in my life. From now on, she wavers between two poles: private and public, inside and outside, and so into the very hollow of life itself. At one time, we are someone's daughter, another time, we are someone's wife, then we become the flower of another who remains other to us. Is there ever hope of belonging to oneself? To speak of a simple illusion wouldn't be any better. The hollow of life, the angular stone of our existence. Alone in the world, sheltered in our refuge, Siliki and I are partners confiding in each other about the futility of love and hate. We construct our public and private space as we see fit. We are in the thick of life.

Siliki speaks to Ada, who seems a bit desperate: "It's because of love and hate that I'm Siliki. I left the unremitting universe of Fulani men to rejoin my spiritual life with the Mafa because for me nothing else seemed able to erase the scandal of useless suffering, to expunge the accumulated sorrow of my story. You know, Ada, I am Siliki because I decided it myself. I want you to be you, to understand life as it comes. I am with you, I am in you. I often see you looking uneasy, and it makes me smile. I want to teach you what I know. I love nature and live in nature. I abandoned the human race a long time ago. Here in this refuge, I breathe and live out my desires. Give me your hand. Listen to the wind outside. Do you hear it? Listen. I want you to learn to understand nature's movements. There are so many signs. I'm tired. I've already seen so many troubles in my life that now, I invent beauty. Don't worry: I'll guide you in this adventure. Beauty is invented, cultivated."

Ada loves precious moments like this when Siliki talks to her. Siliki is always working, either in her garden or at some spiritual activity, like reading, painting, or writing, reflection. Since she loves nature, she always finds a spare moment to mix colors and paint the calabashes in the garden. Writing represents peace of mind for her, but also a way of attaining a certain continuity with her mother's unfinished texts and of melting into the same mold that writing offers to being. For her part, Ada learns how to understand the texts that she calls sacred: "mama's writing." I'm joking, I mean sacred works like the Bible, the Qur'an, and others. She also tells me that the transmission of culture is good for the self. Siliki knows so many things, and Ada doesn't really understand how she succeeded in gaining so much knowledge. She imagines that this woman the villagers call a witch is actually a ball of light.

Ada believes all these cultural transactions are like large oily stains that a boiling soup leaves on pagnes discolored by the sun. She applies herself obediently to everything that Siliki tries to teach her. Her Baba never thought that school was a good thing for a girl, plus Ada was born cursed. But now at least she is learning how to read and write like her brothers who, from time to time, would give her lessons. In spite of the little difficulties that present themselves, her whole heart is in it, and she makes an effort for her beloved. Their relationship solidifies with the passing time. They live there in the refuge, esteemed by the nature that surrounds them.

In the evening, seated next to the fire under a full moon, they listen to the inhabitants of the night. Siliki teaches her to recognize the different nocturnal cries, in particular the hissing serpent, but also the green locust. At night, the Mafa village becomes peaceful; the absence of villagers purifies the atmosphere. The silence blends into their prolonged moments of intimacy. Siliki carries a mountain of tenderness and friendship within her. They spend hours listening to the music produced by their bodies. Rays of sunlight brush against their sleeping faces which reflect back a gentle calm. The dawn breeze and the roosters with their aggressive crowing awaken, as if all of nature were against their conspiring to sleep late into the morning. Like every morning, Siliki slowly heads to the pool on her torso to bathe. She adores the water on her body but never washes the stinking fabric with which she clothes herself. She has developed a sense for strong smells, and so she has an attachment, a vice almost, for the smell of her rags. She takes care of her body so delicately, but not those pieces of stinking fabric.

All of Siliki's little gestures inspire Ada, giving her the courage to look at life in a new light. Their relationship has an existential firmness. They live the present simply—their present, the moment, their delicate moments. It's fortunate that Siliki has joined Ada's life. There were moments of crisis when she couldn't bear the idea of not knowing her past, her mother's story. Siliki, on the other hand, has a past to which she refers rather often. She has solid points of reference, at least that's the sense Ada has gotten about her beloved. Her bitter yet beautiful memories reconstruct her presence and her history, moments that Ada always wants to fix in time. Her fragmented history—the symbol of her life—carries traces that she might recover. How can Ada recover these traces? Siliki surely denotes a point of rupture in her life. Ada's relentless questioning only leads to enigmatic results. She believes that she is definitively nothing more than a succession of traces in the stories of other women. Now that Siliki is in her life, she actually prefers to be one of the traces in Siliki's.

◆◇◆

Day to day, Ada's thoughts trouble her, but fortunately there is peace in her life with Siliki. Like every morning, Siliki is in the water. While Ada lingers in their home, she finds a note attached to her shoes, shoes that Siliki gave her. Siliki understands how essential simple pleasures are. Shoes—what a place to leave a note! That woman is a cynic. The evidence is before Ada that for Siliki, a woman with no legs, shoes have no use. Ada becomes fully aware that she herself has a body whose limbs are all functional. The little note reconstructs a fragment of the story that Siliki's mama left in the packet Siliki received on her wedding day. Siliki has beautiful, careful handwriting: "Here is a piece of obscure information. Read it and tell me what you think. I love you, my sweet friend, my little Ada!"

The notion of appropriation disturbs me. During their capture, future slaves are shut up in compartments. The captives receive the initials of the ship-owner marked with a red-hot iron on their shoulders and are packed into the compartments, laid out body against body. Some women are set aside for the pleasure of the sailors. Thus the voyage begins, calmly, toward the new world.

In one hand, Ada holds a shoe and in the other, the scrap of paper that she has just read. Reading out loud, the words resound like a raging drum, pound into her entire body: slave, compartment, capture, women. For the first time, she wears the shoes that Siliki offered her and leaves their home at a run toward the pool where Siliki goes to collect herself.

The fresh morning air gives her momentum and nature smiles at her, yet everything around their domain is strange that day. Ada doesn't suspect a thing. She runs as fast as she can because she misses Siliki and is dying to tell her that she loves her and what her impressions were after reading the slip of paper. Her step is nimble as she imagines all the gestures she will make when they meet. She will place a kiss on Siliki's forehead and then they will exchange their ideas on the note. Ada recalls the previous evening when she was so exhausted that she fell asleep without giving Siliki a kiss. The whole day had passed like a torrent of water. Concentrated on mixing colors, Ada had tried to paint a calabash that she wanted to offer to Siliki. Sitting all day in a corner of the yard, Ada had stopped feeling her body and lain down. She fell right asleep. The night she passed was sweet and calm, not troubled at all, although it still seemed rather short. All these thoughts parade through her mind as she hurries to reach the pool. When she arrives, she heads to the rock where the two of them often pass long moments together. Siliki isn't there. Ada approaches the pool where Siliki loves to let the bust of her portly body float in the disgusting water. Ada doesn't see her face and is overcome with fear, but a proverb she used to hear in the village comes back to her: "Never lament someone before the time of mourning." Ada suddenly surges into motion when her eyes fall on Siliki's body, lying just on the other side of the rock. Ada starts to scream Siliki's name: Siliki, Siliki, sweet friend! She leans over her to listen for her breathing. Dressed in all her usual rags, it's impossible to detect the faintest beating in her chest. Ada cries, laments and laments alone in the face of her destiny. Emptiness. Loss. Solitude. Her throat clenched, she immediately heads to the village to get help. The ease with which she manages to return to the village without attracting any suspicion encourages her. Seeing her Baba's courtyard again means not only that she must be ready for any and everything but also that she must seize her last hope—the irreversible moment in Siliki's story. No, her return is not another version of the return of the prodigal son, but rather the inscription of a potential rupture. For her Baba, the question of marrying Ada off was never considered. They say Ada resembles her mother too much and no man would want to marry her, even without having to pay a bride price. Anyway, she can see perfectly well that her Baba isn't interested in her. Whenever he comes back from his long trips, he asks for news of his other daughters, whom he calls his pearls.

"How are my jewels doing? I hope they're being guarded just as preciously as they deserve." The patriarch has dug undulating furrows in which to place each of his pearls.

Ada does not figure among them.

◆◇◆

Silence reigns in the village. The sight of mango trees covered with beautiful yellow and red fruit assures me that some village children will be under them. A sense of urgency quickens my pace. Gogo recognizes Ada from afar and lets the others around him know. Ada gesticulates to signal to Gogo, who then runs to her. Gogo and Ada are friends; they used to gather green mangos together. Ada and Gogo like each other without really knowing each other. They have their little secrets that they don't share with anyone else.

They're part of Baba's big courtyard like all the other children. Gogo appreciates Ada's simplicity and smile. He's Ada's favorite. She takes him by the hand and tells him brusquely: "No questions. Go quickly and find my brothers. Discretion is a must. I trust your imagination, but they need to be here within minutes."

Gogo disappears like lightning. The other children, disgusted by Ada's presence, don't know what to do. Talk to her? Spit on her? Confusion sets in. The children's surprise is a good sign for Ada, for she realizes that she hasn't entirely disappeared from the village's memory. Astounded, silent, their eyes wide open, they form a circle around her. All that is audible is the buzzing of flies forever seeking out the scabious sores that cover the legs of some of the children. Ada's two brothers exhibit indescribable tenderness toward her. In no time, one of them appears, happy to see her. He squeezes her in his arms. Without losing a moment, Ada informs him of her misfortune and the help she needs. The scar that emphasizes a being's hybridity begins to bleed again after it's barely healed, and so on for eternity.

Ada hastily explains the situation Siliki is in and asks him to come to the pool with her. "I think that Siliki fell ill, and if you can carry her to our little home, it will be easy to take care of her. She weighs too much for me."

My brother asks me if I still know how to run like when we were little. My brothers taught me how to run and do other useful things. When they had some project, that is to say some dirty trick to play, I was always part of the company. My brother sees my shoes and asks me, "Since when do you wear shoes? Not only are they the perfect representation of subtle torture, but they deform your feet, your body, your personality as a Fulani woman. Flat feet are pretty, and men here like them." He smiles as he slaps me on the shoulder. "Take off those shoes for me, quick. No, I won't let you do it. Put them back on. Take back your body. Quick, let's get going."

He takes me by the hand and, like a shooting star, we charge straight to the rock where poor Siliki is still flat on her back. Her drenched body, slick from fever, makes my heart beat wildly. My brother jumps in fright when he sees Siliki on the ground. He hesitates for a moment: how can he touch this witch, this body that represents abjection itself?

Ada turns toward her brother and speaks to him gently: "This is my dearest. I love her. I want her to live another few hours, minutes, seconds for me. Please, help me. This is just a cry of desperation from someone in love. She isn't dangerous. She won't hurt you. You can carry her."

"Your friend's odor is a little strong."

"It's only a smell, the smell of her rags. I can't explain it, I just love her, that's all." My brother, his jaw agape, doesn't have time to prevent a fly from getting in his mouth. He clearly wants to say something, but Ada pushes him toward Siliki and explains to him calmly, "It's my share of fire! Hurry, hurry!" Moved by the tenderness of my tears, my brother finally takes Siliki in his arms. We head toward our little refuge.

Ada swiftly attends to Siliki, whispering in her ear. She notices a sign of life: Siliki's lips which return a timid smile. Ada asks her brother to go look for plants to prepare a hot drink that will give Siliki back her strength. Meanwhile, Ada gives her water and sponges her forehead while she whispers sweet words. Astounded by these images, my brother is fascinated by our life. Indeed, pleasure is born out of conflict, not out of any kind of unity. Pleasure is learned; it must be chosen and meditated upon, for the conscience is constantly destroyed, annihilated by all the limitations and contradictions surrounding life. Ada asks her brother some questions because she wants to know what's been happening in the village without her. She also asks why her other brother isn't there. Ada's brother promises to come back with their younger brother to visit Siliki. He takes his leave by pinching her nose good-naturedly, a sign of affection and acceptance.

◆◆◆◆

Despite all my attentions, Siliki's condition doesn't improve. She remains exhausted and unable to eat. Night and day, Ada watches at the bedside of their love nest, her hand in Siliki's. She fears death, the eternal flight.

Vain illusions for Ada! There's no need to insist: it's easy to imagine the distress caused by Siliki's illness. Faced with these events, Ada's deep demoralization gets worse and worse. Calm has left her for good. One morning, exhausted from lack of sleep, all of her senses are awakened by the rooster's cry, and she can distinguish each minute detail of its long crows—a brusque reveille that plunges her into hope. Siliki sees more rays of sunlight through the slats in the door. The lack of sleep hasn't affected her sensitivity. Ada experiences a twinge in her heart when she suddenly observes a light smile on Siliki's lips; the same shivers of anguish and hope buried deep in Ada erupt violently again. In her heart of hearts, she is suffering, for Ada is afraid of finding herself alone. In the village, she saw some people disappear into death and others fall into the oblivion of sorrow. Siliki's smile means everything. She repeats it again: she fears death, the eternal flight. She has so many more things to say to Siliki, to learn from her. Siliki, tender friend, you must continue to tell me stories. I will tell them in turn. If you don't write stories down, you forget certain details. Ada had amassed too many stories during the days she spent with Siliki. Her head became a treasure chest where they are all stored. Filled to the brim, memory is short; it is elsewhere, in other spaces that must be found.

Compel yourself to write in order to conserve these stories, Ada tells herself—but how? Even if writing is impossible in the context, one must nevertheless undertake it. Siliki—for days, weeks, months—taught her how to write. And for her, writing is first and foremost a physical act: the contact of hand with pencil, where the hand vigorously imprints a trace, forms a letter, an assemblage of letters to carry on the composition of sacred texts, stories of women. Doesn't the hand remain a neutral instrument in the service of thought, the expression of feelings, the pleasure of communication, to assure the production of stories, even if they are impossible for others to understand? Why do it? Ada asks herself. Impossibility, interdiction, and absence are inscribed in the stories that Siliki tells. Writing is subject to law—for Siliki, the law of the sun, since for her the sun embodies transparency laden with mystery. The sun dries and conserves the ink. With writing, one loses the power of speech, and muteness becomes the watchword; one knows all the while that what writing gains in power, it loses in innocence. Thus the importance for Siliki of the sun's transparency. Writing is like a germinating body out of control: the proliferation of signs that are invoked evoke a certain cowardice. The fact that one encloses oneself in a labyrinth of words poses a heap of problems. But that doesn't matter, for in the case of Siliki and Ada, it's not merely by chance that they remain fixed there over time, in the hollow of the text. This hollow is a refuge, a secret domain for some, but for others it's abjection that pushes them over the edge, into the abyss.

Ada loses herself in all sorts of thoughts. Disgust dries up in her mouth, cowardice engulfs her in inertia. Since the disaster is irreversible, Ada prepares herself, like a beast ready to bolt at any moment. She watches the labyrinth of her life transform into a hazy mirror where it is impossible to distinguish the form of her face. Erasure is the only possibility remaining. Because their story exists in a text—is fixed there—Ada believes she simply needs to understand the dénouement of all the symbols of resistance that have protected her body until now. Siliki once told her how important it is to sculpt violent words onto her skin. The hollow of the text always loses its strength, but a woman's text—a text that inscribes her pain—is powerful. A woman's written story is not at all saturated; on the contrary, this writing is animated by the sign of survival, the symbolics of life where language is traced. In this way, Siliki's writing marks flight, the only convention within our reach. Flight is a fruitful distancing that allows the recollection of fragments and traces. Since Siliki can no longer really talk with Ada, she shuts herself up in infinite whispers.

◆◇◆

Weeks pass with the same brilliant sun, the same rays penetrating through every hole in the hut. But Siliki, who is still confined to bed, no longer shows any hope of life. Only her big eyes bulge out of her head and stare at Ada's to fix them in the void. Then one night, a raging rain threatens the hut, indifferent to Siliki's suffering. It falls all night, the drops drumming against the roof. This violent rain signifies something whose existence we question: the blending of life with death. The night and the rain come to an end under the sign of Siliki's death. The breath of that union affirms the rupture: on one side, the rain stops falling, its melody is extinguished; and on the other side, a new day rises, and the shutters of misery open boldly despite the void. Ada is alone now. The bell of her life has tolled: solitude. Her only hope is to disappear into the void. This non-fulfillment—the gulf between the said and the unsayable—haunts the wisdom that Siliki has passed on to Ada. Siliki's speech is also extinguished into nothing, beyond an elsewhere. What sorrow! That woman, that Siliki, represents love itself. In giving love and tenderness, she showed Ada the essential. How does one love human beings and nature, feel a human heart beating, laugh, cry, fight, rise up, suffer, overcome, believe, study, live and participate in everything that lives in nature and in one's heart? Her generosity of spirit truly touched Ada. She taught her to see herself as a woman, a woman who loves herself and is capable of loving another woman.

◆◇◆

Ada and her two brothers provided a funeral worthy of Siliki. Like the pictures she loved to paint, her modest casket was covered with all the flowers in her domain. Siliki, who was passionate about nature and her world, was attended by the calm of the pool and some passing seagulls who glided along the swell of water, leaving an amber wake behind them. Snakes, birds, fish, caimans, roosters, hens, goats, bees, butterflies—all of nature was present for the meditation. A member of their community was starting off on the voyage of no return. All was silent in the nature she would never see again. Her tomb was delicately prepared next to the rock, the only place worthy of receiving Siliki. Whereas both of them used to spend hours daydreaming by the water at Siliki's final resting place, from now on Ada would spend her time there alone. Because Ada had Siliki buried close to the rock by the pool, not far from their dwelling, she can still spend a lot of time with her there; her spirit will remain near her love, Ada. Ada is the one who is still alive, so she clothes herself in their love, the only clothing that merits their dignity. The wound that had barely healed is bleeding anew, and the pain of it makes Ada suffer. There are moments when Ada contemplates death. She dreams of death gently, exactly like a clock marking time: each second, minute, hour that passes leaves the weight of solitude behind. All these thoughts center around the illusion of human community, yet Ada feels she is the only one crying for Siliki. She knows that all of nature will be melancholy, but her own melancholy will be of an archaic kind. It touches something much deeper. After all, she has lost her one love, sweet Siliki, gone in silence, the silence of the dead. She had often told her about silence, but the silence of the living. Sadness invades Ada as the day draws out. She swims in the sum of her memories, beautiful memories of love with a legless woman in stinking rags. Ada recalls those odors that she misses already. Siliki's body bore a magnet, which perhaps evaporated in her inert body, that attracted Ada to her. Ada is wrapped up in her world, in her passion. After all, life is, above anything else, debauchery of the imagination. During the weeks that Siliki has been absent, Ada has lived in the company of a dream, a vision that almost never leaves her.

✦◇✦◇✦

To die because she can no longer bear to live is one solution, but a cowardly one. Especially with a destiny traced at the back of the shadows like hers, Ada must live. Quite simply, she has to continue to break divides. Submission, even of the symbolic kind, is the rule of the game. Siliki initiated her, bended and unbended her like a liana vine. Now Ada must consummate the act, that is to say, she must bring forth all this interiorization. The only thing she has is her body, her only form of resistance; nothing can change that mark. She understands now the worth of things to which she assigns almost no importance. Siliki taught her the classical corpus, including languages, reading, painting, and many secrets of traditional Mafa culture. Siliki never asked Ada's opinion. She projected Ada into the act, just as her inscription invited her into it. She drew up lists of classic texts that one must know for a certain form of survival. She often adopted an ironic air when she pronounced that word: survival. How to survive? The process seemed endless to her, but with Siliki, one didn't question the challenge, for these two women are themselves a challenge—the type of challenge that is constituted before one even becomes aware what a challenge is. Ada reproduced all the gestures perfectly. Maybe love controls everything. In any case, there is an eye somewhere, watching. Siliki used to watch Ada for long periods with a grimace on her face. She had mastered certain foreign languages that she in turn taught Ada, making her repeat the words with care. When Siliki taught her to read, everything had to be respected perfectly, each intonation supervised, placed at the correct time: there is a harmony in convention that must not be touched, just like in theatre if you want the role to achieve its full effect. To give her a concrete example, Siliki told her a story that was actually a secret she was supposed to understand, keep for herself, furtively benefit from one day, and finally pass on to another woman.

In Fulani tradition, the tradition of my parents, every young girl must prove her virginity to the secret society of women, which basically means to the entire culture. For the mothers, it's a source of real drama, a grave affront if their daughters have betrayed them. Raised in a milieu where rape and the sexual act are confused, mothers who are worried about the double shame that can destroy a family give all kinds of advice to their daughters. In short, it's a path that couldn't be any more typical for a young girl. In my case, I was deflowered stupidly in a family dispute because virtue among our people remains a necessity. Make love or be raped—as if in a mold, these two concepts blend into each other, and no one in the village clearly understands the difference. From time to time, people talk about rape, but only when an old man rapes his little five-year-old niece. One of my sisters, the victim of one or the other, didn't know how to distinguish between them herself. Deflowered by a neighbor who wasn't about to come forward, my father demanded the performance of the verification of all the daughters living under his roof. In my case, the banana went very far into my body and tore me without any trouble. How barbaric, to be deflowered in public by a banana. Having committed the act and seeing so much blood come from between my legs, my father lowered his eyes filled with woe but not any shame. I, on the other hand, was so ashamed in front of all those people that I felt my heart stop for a second. Seized by shame after this act of collective rape, I knew that I had just been mutilated, exactly like all women in our culture, and the silence on this subject won me over for all time.

◆◇◆

But my mother whispered ideas into our ears. A safety pin is your leech; it won't leave you, and you don't let go of it until it's served its purpose. You have to be aware that in rituals, what counts is to play along; the act becomes symbolic. So at night, while my husband proved himself a believer in the ritual that consisted of getting off in a mix of pleasure and pain, I shoved the safety pin into various places in my flesh that felt neither pleasure nor pain to produce blood. I shoved that safety pin into my fingers, my arms, my legs; it didn't matter where, for the next morning I would be clothed up to the neck and no one would see my body. As for blood, there was plenty of it, and my mother and I were honored in our representation of Fulani women. Not being deflowered of one's human dignity, that's what the stakes were. All these memories must be inscribed between *quotation marks*, just like our history; its absence signifies destiny. The white margins, the blank space, are where one can find the efforts of a consciousness that throws itself cheerfully into a siege of the world, dodging contradictions and symbolic gestures in order to represent this history. All of this can only be understood as a rift of human history's strangeness and disorder. History remains catastrophic. Everyone must reconstruct it in their own way: succinctly, adding, pasting words back together, fragments of sentences between quotation marks . . . and so on for infinity.

Ada thinks back on Siliki's stories and how she often listened to them without comment. Then, as if she'd taken a wrong turn, Ada's head bumps into her habitual solitude. There is no reason for anything to change. It's just the melancholy of an overcast day; the days end and fade away into the void like death itself. The symbolic death of these sad days touches Ada deeply. She feels herself dying in her solitude. This time, she is well and truly alone, serene, sitting on the rock next to Siliki's grave where she has just deposited a pretty bouquet of flowers. Flowers give her pleasure because they contain natural fragrances, incense that penetrates to the source, beyond the depths of a life's mystery. Siliki used to say that the source is the true site of combat, the combat led by the empire of wild imagination, the combat spilling over with all the other combats governing the world. The source is an odd turmoil that invades your heart of hearts. The source is a pleasure, a sadness, feelings that you experience alone in the deepest hollows. In Ada's case, the source is hatred that reopens her scar, barely healed, and makes it bleed anew. Tears cover her face. What a void without Siliki! Sobs slowly strangle Ada. She knows that, one day, she will go to join her beloved. If silence remains present in the face of despair, it's no surprise that the Word becomes the key to the other side, her destiny. So Ada writes little messages that she reads to Siliki, which leads her to recall their moments together and reassures her to some degree. Not only does it plunge her into the delights of writing, but it also allows her to convey all the sweet thoughts that slip into the text she carefully crafts to take to Siliki. Words forge the kernel of love, more intimately than light forges the day. Words overflow from every side of the project and the act of writing itself. Writing is a deviation that causes suffering— even though that suffering gives a certain pleasure, so that you are no longer victim to suffering, especially when you master the language of the other.

When Ada arranges words to give them what is proper to their substance—that is to say, the void that gives birth to speech—her sadness mingles with joy and incites her to produce even more beautiful texts that will leave traces for her Siliki who knew how to live the depths of the soul. Certain desperate days, at the end of hot afternoons, she gathers a pretty bouquet of flowers and carries it to Siliki with a little text that she reads with great difficulty as emotion strangles her words: *"The gaze of a woman blind from birth who has never looked at herself in the mirror, has never been reflected in another's gaze, is the only face that is pure of all comedy, of all indulgence, for it usually puts one ill at ease. Fortunately, this blind woman has the profound gaze of a soul who understands."*

When she returns to their refuge, she walks slowly to make the most of the marvels of the setting sun. Their domain is beautiful and peaceful. On the quiet path, the glow of the timid twilight sun becomes clearer. Birds dispatch cries of greeting from the distance. The hut is quiet. The little lamp projects rays of light into the small space entirely mutilated by silence. Ada wraps herself up in one of the many pagnes that Siliki had piled on a stone. Of all Siliki's pagnes, Ada takes out this one, on which she had painted various figures and marks. She caresses a corner of the pagne a long, long, long time with teardrops that slide between her fingers. It's dreadful to realize that she must speak of the past at present. Ada wavers between past and present. I love Siliki—no, I loved her. But in any case, I still love her. How heartrending! The loss remains, and no matter how much time passes, it does nothing to change the tragedy. Ada's scar, barely healed, bleeds anew. The lingering wound reminds her that the person she loved so much is now absent. Everything in their refuge signifies that absence. Ada feels as though she is in an abyss of love's indissociable violence and powerlessness. Powerlessness or impossibility remain the obstacles in the whole adventure. Fate. A dangerous word. Danger is inevitable, and therein lies the conflict. Ada is drunk with the desire to act, but what can she really do? This idea has become unbearable to her. Siliki left her all by herself in a closed vase from which she will never emerge. Ada often awakens stunned, sometimes frightened, but she refuses to remember dreams where interdiction holds sway.

◆◇◆

The moon spills its light throughout the hut. The glow of the little kerosene lamp and the intermingled odors that remind her of Siliki keep Ada company. It seems impossible to her to erase the memory of tenderness. Pain sears her body, and silence penetrates her and leaves the taste of nothing in her inert mouth. Her body is heavy with sorrow; she feels only a tickle in her fingers. She has the impression that the kind of piquant spices that tear through the body are permeating her fingers and disturbing her as deeply as the void left by the death of the being so dear to her. Her fingers, which nourish her with the fruits of life, have coagulated. She feels heavy, and all of her limbs are aching.

The fascination and horror that Siliki's past evokes—in fact that her entire life inspires in me—does not come simply from her person but from the whole enigma linked to the other who is also my self. By mimicking the everyday, Siliki succeeded, in her unique way, in problematizing her role in the comedy, first of Fulani society and then Mafa society, where her soul now reposes. Her history is marked down between quotation marks in the history that includes traces of invisible filth, erased from the body but present in the mind. Siliki made those traces appear elsewhere, precisely in the places where interdiction leaves its breath: the mind, memory.

As an expression of love, Ada immerses herself for hours on end in the texts that Siliki left behind. Like her mother, Siliki wrote on everything she found lying about, everything that could absorb ink without it disappearing. That's why the sun was important to her. The sun did everything. The effacement and reinscription of traces embellish the charter of our tale. Wise and practical women: encrust words, speech, and signs everywhere the void leaves its tragedy; in no way must indifference allow forgetfulness. How can we forget all these events which mark our time? It would be ridiculous to prepare a list, for history is long and does not deserve to be evaded in this way. History takes charge of its own avenues. The symbol of the women's liberation movement is surely the act of speaking out in every form. Siliki, with her elusive pen sharpened by her revelatory mistrust and her constant revolt, had illuminated the margins between certain people's dreams and other people's reality. She wrote, but because she acted lucidly, she remained wary of the failings of writing, which touts itself like a prostitute or politician.

Indeed, if you add too many modifications, the quotation marks become unwieldy and impede the act of reading. Shutting up and bending their backs in submission—that's what Fulani women were capable of in the face of the threatening signs lying in wait for them.

It is cool in the hut as the wind blows hard and deafening rumbles reverberate in the sky. The atmosphere is restless; a storm is threatening. Absorbed in her reading, Ada's thoughts wander through the texts, and she travels, projects herself into ineffable lands. Suddenly, a raging wind begins to blow through the trees, and the endless sound of cracking tears her from her reading. Bent over on the bench, she starts to cry for her love. She isn't even able to drown herself in the beautiful memories so close at hand. The hut hasn't changed at all since Siliki's death. Ada wants to keep everything in its original place. Everything around her is sad and dreary. Limp, confused, she slides into their love nest where Siliki's old pagnes—the only witnesses to her solitude—are warm. In her heart of hearts, Ada knows that the love of her sweet friend is protecting her. She is overcome by a light, gentle mood, and she decides to read the poems that Siliki wrote.

◆◇◆◇◆

A breaker wave of images that tantalizes my body. Oh! Poetry in pidgin—but why? Ada can read a few words, but not the poems as a whole. Pidgin is spoken, but she didn't know that you could actually write in this dialect. Siliki has always been and always will be surprise itself. Even after her death, she continues to intrigue me. There must be some explanation. She often said that you should be suspicious of escape routes that seem too easy. She signed her poems "Silk" and her other texts "Like," when she didn't forget to sign them entirely, for there were too many bits of text without an addressee, no name or signature. With beautiful descriptions, she had written her mother's story, which Ada tried in turn to restore here, of course with the guilty conscience of a translator who appropriates another's words for herself. Siliki the dragonfly's poetry—light and inspired—has magical wings that transport Ada to vibrantly colored lands and tickle our imagination into action. Ada continues to read. She moves from discovery to discovery. Every day her experience is enriched further, though unfortunately she has no one with whom to share the pleasure.

Curiosity prevents Ada from attending to any other affairs. She spends her days in the hut reading the notes that Siliki had tucked away in various objects. She discovers a story that pleases her enormously. She experiences so much pleasure from reading the story that she finds herself once again in the clouds of Siliki's thought. Since the morning is hot, she leaves the hut with the story that she will read for Siliki. Reading Siliki's writing changed her life. There's something very strange about reading. Her brothers know how to read because they went to school like all the boys in Baba's household. Her brothers tried to teach her to read and write without much success. It must be said that in their Baba's household, this kind of activity is a waste of time and effort. But with Siliki, Ada managed to learn the necessity of the act of reading that then encourages the act of writing. She is still in front of the hut as these thoughts jostle around in her head. Though hot, the morning air is fresh. Everything around their dwelling is calm, as if to celebrate some special homage. Ada walks around the hut for several minutes to breathe the morning air then heads toward Siliki's tomb where she will settle in to read to her the text she loves so much. The text, in fact, written by Siliki.

◆◇◆◇◆

In the middle of beautiful prairies there was a beautiful estate. Slender palm trees surrounded the numerous huts like vigilant, seasoned guards. The banana trees solemnly tossed their large shredded leaves in the breeze's breath. A young missionary lady was riding on a narrow path in the middle of tall grass. That day she wanted to go to the king's private secretary's field to talk to him—to him and his wives—about Godly things. She was deep in her thoughts for she knew that this estate was reputed in the whole village to be a bastion of paganism, superstition, and witchcraft. However, the owner was an intelligent man who lived according to the rigorous principles of Fulani tradition. He possessed a large, beautiful property with thirty women at his disposal. He never ate or drank anything without first sacrificing some of his food or palm wine to the spirits of the dead. In his beautiful room embellished with all sorts of decorations presented to him by his wives, there was a hollow in the ground next to his mat which served as a dish for sacrifices to the dead. When he washed his hands before a meal, he would regularly place boiled corn, meat, and palm oil sauce in the sacrifice dish and pour a little palm wine on top, saying in prayer, "To those who are under the earth and to the Gods!" He venerated many

Gods. Each tree and bush was inhabited, according to him, by supernatural beings, and the murmur of springs and brooks seemed to him to be the language of the God of water. He had enormous respect for the God of water, because of the rain he needed for his many fields. In those fields, divine beings frolicked, and he protected his estate from their evil spells with fetishes that could be seen above every door. No God he knew was good or benevolent. All the ones he venerated were mean, deceitful, cruel beings who tormented humans by sending them worries, illnesses, and misfortunes in their fields and homes.

Among the many wives of this poor man, a dozen had converted to Christianity and had been baptized for some time. He had not prevented them in any way, which was surprising. Maybe he loved them after all and so gave them a little freedom, or maybe quite simply he was upright in his religious principles, for he firmly believed that there were many Gods. The Christians with their stars on their heads didn't have an easy life on his estate, though, because the other women made fun of them and made their life bitter by any means possible. Sister Gertrude knew this, and it was for this reason that she visited the women often. Sister Gertrude was always cordially received on the estate. The owner himself conducted the little white woman into the garden behind his house and called his Christian wives. Almost always, it was only the baptized wives who came; the others found some pretext for being absent from the property. Time spent with these Christians was rather agreeable and salutary. Sister Gertrude always ended her visits by solemnly repeating, "May peace be with you, my daughters. Alleluia."

Little by little, Sister Gertrude entered deeply into the lives of the Christian women on the estate and obtained permission to take them out for various activities at the mission. The Catholic mission was on top of a hill that overlooked the village. It was a rather pleasant estate, surrounded by gardens maintained by thousands of Christians humbled by their faith. A little stream ran along the giant rocks that smothered the cries and tears that escaped from the village, which was often in a state of crisis. The land was fertile around the mission: papaya, mango, avocado, orange, lemon, plum, cherry, and palm trees whetted the appetite at every turn as the exotic fruits formed a colorful ensemble.

The Christian women's visits to the mission became regular. Sita Sophie, a wife whose nickname was "gazelle" because of her long neck, went to the mission almost every day and spent countless hours there. Sita Sophie was the portrait of Christian conquest. She had metamorphosed so quickly, faster than a chameleon, that she gained a new nickname—"Chameleonia"— from her jealous co-wives. The women in the residence were clothed in long, straight, rather ample dresses that many of them wore rather gracefully. They went barefoot, and up top they wore a large kerchief folded into a triangle and rolled fancifully around their heads. Every day, Chameleonia changed her headscarf, which Sister Gertrude slipped to her in secret. It wasn't only headscarves that contributed to Chamelonia's metamorphosis, it was also her attitude: she seemed light, radiant with her smile. Her sleepy gazelle look softened more each day. To look at her, one saw love in her eyes. The intoxication of pleasure that her body enjoyed rendered her beautiful, delicious enough to eat. Sita Sophie did not evoke so much a woman as yet another animal, one known for its modesty: the heifer. She smiled politely but was clearly dumb-founded by the charged jokes of her co-wives who were troubled by her impenetrable character.

But her discretion remained the key to all her mysteries. She spent a particularly large amount of time with Sister Gertrude. The two women developed a special friendship, and from then on, they went to preach the good news together. One was clothed in a large blue dress, tinted by the harsh dry seasons; the other wore a gandoura embroidered with lively colors. Light-footed, they advanced like butterflies through the furrows in the fields. All along their path through the expanse of fields, they entertained themselves with the kinds of things that one would ascribe to lovers. Caressed by the light warm afternoon wind, they stretched out on the grass and whispered sweet nothings. Gently, gently, their hands slid over breasts, stomachs, and further down until they touched serenity. They laughed softly with the pleasure that this touch supplied them. They made sure to hide themselves well in the grass so that passersby wouldn't surprise their games of love and seduction. Sister Gertrude, Hungarian by birth, had spent her childhood in Hungary, then in Canada where she had decided, after her theological studies, to leave for black Africa. She had so particular a passion for Sita Sophie— this woman with feline allure—that she ended up enclosing her in the shadows of her heart. She gave her lessons in reading, writing, painting, music, sewing, and sexuality. Sister Gertrude reproduced her entire education on this Chameleonia. Because of their strong feelings for each other, their work quickly developed quite an assiduous rhythm. They spent whole days in the mission library. Sister Gertrude first taught Chameleonia Greek and Latin without much success, but at least she arrived at certain basics of a classical education. Nothing had dissipated from Sister Gertrude's Western methodology: "The path of the masters of this world is the path to follow. Greek and Latin will be very useful because they're the key to sacred texts." There was no mystery to this reasoning. The theory remained fluid, and Sister Gertrude—so refined in her approach to scholastics—was convinced of the good she was doing for humanity. Yet the remarks that came from Sister Gertrude were often cynical. Her singular impressions, the disjointed and undefined expressions of her thought, motivated Chameleonia to uncover the mystery of this evangelical adventure. According to her co-wives, Sita Sophie had been barely fourteen years old when she was married, in exchange for a large bride price, to the owner of the superb residence, the forsaken hermit of the world where Sister Gertrude had eventually landed. Sita Sophie had lived in utter sadness, despite the limpid sky that brightened her days. She was lacking almost everything: love, tenderness, her parents, even a part of her body. Like all the young girls in her village, she had undergone infibulation without much protest.

It was the first time Sister Gertrude had touched the body of a woman without a clitoris. And it was the first time that Sita Sophie had experienced real sexual pleasure. Sister Gertrude felt so bad for Sita Sophie that she tried to provide other forms of pleasure that would make her companion bloom. When Sister Gertrude, like a burning sun, smiled at her through the good word, the luminosity of her speech distinctly projected into Sita Sophie's head the long silent film of her life up till then: only great waves of anguish and internal torments! Her feelings of humiliation remained confused. Sister Gertrude could no longer do without Sita Sophie. In the flowering fields under the big gray dress of a nun adrift, her dust-covered white sandals outlined her little tanned feet. Murmuring timidly, she wandered the streets of the Fulani village in search of a glance from Chameleonia, the one who now bore the name of her enigma and the malaise of living out her feelings. Sometimes her

husband punished her by shutting her up or assigning her difficult tasks like drawing water a long ways away and other
chores whose description is best left unsaid, so humiliating
are they for every woman. Silence forms part of the world of
unmoving violence. Sister Gertrude accompanied her to the
edge of the village to draw water. It was a pleasure for the two
of them since they could have fun along the way. Fleeing all the
contradictions of their lives, they could rediscover the calm that
the countryside along their path offered. They stayed lying in
the soft grass until the beginnings of dusk. Under the setting
sun, their evenings were long and sweet. Lying in the grass, the
first fresh chill of twilight nipped the skin of their bare legs, but
it also signaled their return to the village. Going back slowly,
they often thought about the consequences of their relationship
in their respective milieus. Sister Gertrude would say good-
naturedly to Sita Sophie, "My sweet friend, it must be said.
Abomination! Desolation! Scandal! This affair is embarrassing. They're two women, one from the snowy country, the
other from sun-drenched lands. How morbid: two women in
love with each other, one white and one black. The worst is
that on top of all this scandal, one of them is a nun, a bearer of
the great civilizing mission under the auspices of the Catholic
Church!" They would burst into laughter and embrace, thinking of the latest separation that awaited them at the entrance to
the mission.

The secret relationship between Sita Sophie and Sister Gertrude was discovered, leaving deep and lasting traces in the
village. Of course, Sister Gertrude could not talk about it because
it was a shocking subject for the Catholic mission. Consumed
by her thoughts as she cleaned her room, Sister Gertrude whispered these harsh words to herself: "In any case, in weather like

this, you can't even go outside without coming back spattered with the thin but stubborn mud of moral commodities. I made up my mind; I live my sexuality. Some people don't like to look at their feet when they walk. Is it a fault to cast your gaze into the distance while the majority are reduced to seeking what's missing from their lives in the most meager sentimental coherence?" Sister Gertrude understood then all the sad vicissitude of life and the complex mechanisms liable to define human beings. But she quietly packed the trunk of books she was giving to Sita Sophie and disappeared without any last-minute embrace. After their initial desire to glorify their relationship with emotional goodbyes, in the end they were without emotion. Everything had become an obstacle. Sister Gertrude left the mission without a word, without a tear, her eyes fixing the void, her throat clenched and dry. She gave off no emotion, for her anguish blocked everything. She felt empty. Sorrow hypnotized her completely. The Catholic community condemned her homosexual acts rather severely and sent her back to Canada. Sita Sophie stayed on the estate where her life would take all kinds of violent turns: she had committed the most vile act, and thus the most humiliating one. Beaten frequently by her husband who demanded a child from her, she had no more words for prayers that only fell back down into the abyss.

After praying so much with no result and losing her love without any explanation, doubt moved into her life. As if in distant dreams, she often heard the sounds and murmur of unknown languages prophesying sweet messages. Her despair was real, for her isolation in the void had become exasperating for her small person. When the decision was taken to throw her into a village for mad people, she became pregnant. Her pregnancy helped to erase her shame, and after that, everything happened according to the norms of her husband's customs. She had a daughter whom she named Siliki, which in Duala means silk, that rare and fragile fabric. Caring for silk requires a certain precision, even a certain delicacy of the soul!

◆◇◆

This is how Siliki bound up all the secrets of her mother who had died in grief but left her daughter the treasure of this earth: knowledge that leads to seeking out one's own path. Her mother had told her this story on scraps of paper and letters, as proof of her love. It was impossible to know how Siliki had acquired all the knowledge left by her mother. Ada doesn't know how Siliki ended up in the Mafa village, or the cause of her physical disability, or where her daughter Affi is. Ada is embarrassed by her curiosity. She wants to know. She experiences this desire as both a right and a necessity in her life.

Describing Ada's interpretation of Siliki and her mother's writing is the same thing as describing the furrows in the monotone life of the women around her. In the rain, their pagnes take on sad, somber colors, like the sadness in their lives that they conjugate in all the tenses of silence; this is the unpleasant truth of their lives. Ada thinks of Siliki with tears in her eyes. She cries because she will never see her again. Sorrow covers her like rain covers trees, houses, and people without umbrellas, yet water slides off her as if she wore a rare kind of raincoat. Oh! sweet Siliki, Ada cries for you in her heart like the rain in the night into which sorrows escape.

A light rain is falling, cleaning the plants and flowers suffering under the daytime sun and dust. Softly, Ada makes out the noise of the drops escaping from the leaves. It's the rainy season, and every time it rains, Ada has the strong impression that the water can carry her to the heart of her own internal search. The water runs into the marshes at a frenzied speed that gives pregnant women dizzy spells. It carries everything in its path on its voyage. The rainy season bears melancholy evenings where only drops of water break the silence. Ada enjoys the evening humidity that propels her into a deep, sometimes cosmic, sleep. Unconsciously, she likes the sweetness and violence of water. Ada often has the impression that life is diluted in what she perceives as water's immobility. Under the rain, she forgets herself, loses herself. The feelings the rain evokes give her a better understanding of her sweet friend Siliki who spent hours swimming in the water, daydreaming in that mysterious backwater pool. For her, that's what living was about; for her, that was life. Losing herself in the immensity of water meant living and rediscovering her soul in a furrow of harmony.

ADA

Fragrant fruits rise from the depths, gently, gently toward Ada; she breathes in the aroma silently, without opening her eyes or her mouth or her hands stretched out in fists. Like a graceful little cat, she extends her arms, her legs, her whole body. But even though she slept as soundly as a kitten, she is still shaken by her visit to the Garba boui-boui. When she thinks of the caretaker and her charming words, she is frankly hesitant to go back, and yet she must.

She continues to roam through the village, standing, sitting, lying down. She wanders like a bird lost in the heavens.

The earth, damp with rain, emits an organic smell that the villagers inhale deeply. The village reposes in its monotony. Silence and despair filter into their emotions. Ada is so tired of searching for a tangled route that promises absolutely nothing, no path leading to hope. Everything makes her anxious, and tears often cover her cheeks. The complexity of fully engaging in the act of refusal has left her weary. Silence comprises the village's daily reality. What misery for lives that are so fragile after all!

After so many trials and tribulations, Ada does not, however, grow weary. Instead, strength comes to her from an unknown source. She thinks of mental asphyxia, which awakens something strong inside her: the will to struggle. She must struggle, and that means getting Affi back in order to get her Siliki back. So Ada ponders the different possibilities that present themselves. Her days sprawl out with worry. She talks to everyone who passes before her. Finally one day, a day like any other, with no sign of hope, she is walking alone, all alone and lost in her thoughts when two women approach her. The women start chattering rapidly, both at the same time. Ada listens but does not react. It's interesting to observe the gestures that accompany the women's words. Squeezed into their pagnes which they adjust around their waists, they remind her of the bickering women in her Baba's extended household. It was truly a sight to see them at it, especially when their pagnes would suddenly slide from their hips and they were exposed to the whole household. The burst of laughter that erupted from the crowd would stop the quarrel. And now she finds herself before two unknown women from her own world filling her head with empty chatter. They talk and talk until they're out of breath.

And Ada, for her part, listens. She is seeing the spectacle of her Baba's courtyard all over again, and that spectacle casts her back into the sad scenes that marked her youth.

It's so hot that the women's faces are covered in sweat, a sweat that nonetheless diffuses a certain luminosity. The heat typically causes the faces of the women in the Fulani village to produce an oily surface in need of constant wiping. Both women wipe their faces with the palms of their hands, and Ada, still silent, observes their every gesture. Calmly, one of them looks her right in the eye and tells her she wants to talk to her about the Garba boui-boui because she's seen Ada hanging around there. She explains that the villagers are a little worried by her presence because they always see her by herself, and they don't understand how a young woman can wander about alone. Always alone. It's rare for Fulani women to walk alone down a path, or even in the village. One of the women continues, "So my friend and I thought it would be a good idea to approach you and have a chat with you. If you want, we can help you since, between women, we understand each other. But you have to talk so we understand what you want around that boui-boui. Don't worry, really—trust us." I listen, guarding my silence and observing their gestures carefully. Then quickly, I take a deep breath and begin to explain my situation, my desires and distress. They listen, this time without saying a word, and I talk and talk without really breathing. Words flow from my mouth like from a wellspring. One of them tells me that it's not such a difficult situation to resolve because she works with people from the outside, that is to say, Westerners who come to the village to do research. The Garba boui-boui has a reputation across the seas and oceans, a real fertile garden for the research of secrets. Of course, I don't understand what they're telling me. I've never heard anyone talk about these Western researchers. The women begin to explain how it works.

Western experts in anthropology, linguistics, and history regularly venture into the village. Unlike us, they have the right to observe the different bouis-bouis in the area for their academic research in order to enrich the register of knowledge about other cultures. I find the abuses produced at every level truly troubling. Our countries, our villages continue to venerate the feats and successes of Western cultures. They're allowed to transgress all the codes of our customs, but we cannot. Their excuse is that they're foreigners and researchers. As she speaks, Nafi becomes full of passion. Sula and I listen without interrupting. Nafi is very pretty, a pleasure to look at. That natural beauty you find from time to time in African villages. Her voice is deep but soft, and respects the rhythm of her sentences. Nafi makes it clear that she will take care of my situation, and her best friend Sula will help because they do everything together, even if the ancestors don't approve. "But luckily for us in this village, we wear a mask to hide ourselves. Now listen carefully, you need to know how the mask works, that's all, and I don't mean just symbolically. Plus, we're in the game, always in the game, so let's play with as few errors as possible." Sula and Nafi burst out laughing, an incredible laugh. I'm already fascinated by how much fun they have together. "Don't fret, Ada. Sula and I are like freshwater fish here. The villagers tolerate us, but that's it."

◆◇◆

"We're going to have you wear the real white mask to infiltrate you into the boui-boui where Affi is. Even if we have to whiten your skin, we have all the soaps and creams to do it. But, dear Ada, you're a black woman with big succulent lips, a flat nose, and lashless eyes shaped like devilish needles. It's not that we lack imagination—some things you just cannot change. Then you have to create." Sula has taken over talking and starts to empty her bag. She talks and talks without taking a breath. This time it's Nafi and I who listen attentively. Sula takes me by the hand, explaining her frustration with everything that happens in the village. I feel Sula's hand in mine. In the heat, sweat slides between our fingers. Sula in turn looks me right in the eyes and asks me to listen carefully: "I personally feel a deep hatred for all these mechanisms. The universal consensus to assault human dignity, the only fine clothing we wear in this world. Dignity. Integrity is another question. The pain we feel has no words; perhaps there is only silence close to its soul and a few visible traces. One has to be humble. These grand principles interest everyone on a philosophical level, but when it comes to their concrete application, the subject gets put on the table for discussion and then just rolls around there. I refuse the matter-of-fact logic that doesn't see anything outside of the usual frame, this life of the wretched of the earth who submit and endure without the slightest hope." At these sordid thoughts, the three of them head for the bus station to negotiate with the new arrivals in the village, which seems peaceful enough. Sula explains what we need to do to infiltrate the boui-boui, but I confess I don't understand everything. Siliki had taught me so much about life that I felt strong and present when faced with critical situations, but the current one with these two women goes beyond my limits. They make me nervous.

Sula thinks I'm a little soft, to the point where she often loses patience. Nafi, on the other hand, understands me and tells me she likes the fact that I'm soft and calm. Sula and Nafi are both back in the village after having spent a long time in the United States where they had tried unsuccessfully to make their fortune. Sula talks too fast and is so worked up that I don't understand what she's trying to explain, but according to Sula I remain soft and calm.

The buses, which arrive every day at irregular hours from the neighboring city, sometimes drop off Western researchers. At the bus station where we three find ourselves, Sula talks to everyone: tourists, missionaries, students, professors, and researchers of all sorts milling around. They come and go, only their clothing distinguishing them from the villagers. Even though the women's ideas about how to proceed seem well developed, some important details escape me. Sula is always making unexpected remarks, and I'm supposed to understand everything. She taps Nafi's shoulder, which makes her jump. Sula explains how her hatred is complex and double. Nafi smiles, tells Sula she knows and gives her all her support. Nafi, her face tensed, explains how she detests all these people who have only one goal, to strip her of her one fine dress: her dignity. Sula calls my name loudly to get my attention. "Ada, listen! Are you listening, Ada?" Sula talks louder and louder. "As far as the Fulani are concerned, their confusion confirms the alienation and foundering of our cultures. And since that's the way it is, I'm taking advantage of this confusion to infiltrate Ada into the boui-boui. If foreigners have the right to multiple visits and as much time as they want, then Ada, too, has the right to the same privileges and observations." Nafi smiles to see her friend Sula so worked up on my behalf.

Ada trembles at the idea of getting to know Affi. There is nothing left that can prevent her from joining her pain to that of Siliki's daughter. Ada fears nothing now.

At the bus station, Sula approaches a couple who look rather young and extremely susceptible to the decor and staging of the scene. Stunned by the locale's usual brou-haha, the young couple are rooted in place, immersed in fear by the reality of our bus stations. Yet the honking horns, bony goats, chickens tied by their legs to suitcases, mothers worried about the improbability of their trips and the sun beating down on the heads of the children strapped to their backs, men in close-fitting, chest-hugging shirts busy with negotiations for the upcoming journeys—all these suggest that the scene is not a sad one. The buses and bush taxis bear all sorts of graffiti and notices reading: "Signed, Death," "King of the Bush," "Down with Speed," "The Driver is King," "Vive la Route," "Rose, you're the one I love," "Beware of Dog," "Come closer, dear, I don't bite," "Bruce Lee, King of the Steering Wheel," "Rocci runs faster than his shadow" and so on. Like a birdsong resounding through a distant forest, startling the ear and demanding complete attention, the anthropologist couple seems lost in the vast movement of the station. At that moment, their ears are pricked up to listen, their eyes wide to observe. The situation is so intense they must pay heed to every gesture. It's true that they had prepared for their journey. They informed themselves about Fulani culture and the cultures of West Africa in general;

they watched documentaries about African adventures. But now, standing before reality, they find that the real is not always transcendent. Lost in the clouds as they are, the irreparable has already been done.

With a smooth, honeyed voice, Sula takes the woman's hand and says, "Can I help you? I'm from here."

Surprised by Sula's intervention, the young woman accompanies her timid words with a little gesture of the head: "We're American researchers. This is my husband Steve, and I'm Kate. And you?"

Sula introduces herself with a light smile, just to show that she too uses Colgate toothpaste every morning to insure those pearly whites, and in a rather cynical tone she says, "I'm Sula, this is my friend Nafi, and this is Ada."

Ada exclaims as if she had just been bitten by a wasp, "It's the name given to me by the mother I never knew. I think she's dead. But since I'm not sure, I look for her everywhere, and this young woman that I have to meet in the Garba boui-boui might be able to help me."

"How indiscreet!" Sula cries. "Why does she need to tell her life story to these strangers?"

Ada speaks up again, this time addressing Sula: "Listen, Sula, my despair has sent me off the rails. I know I'm losing my head. I realize I'm going beyond the limits of what's allowed. Fine, I'm sorry, Sula. I'll be quiet and listen to all the wonderful stories this young couple has to tell us."

All three turn to listen to the young American couple. Ada listens open-mouthed, so surprised is she by their spontaneity. Kate is the one talking, since she has a ready tongue and expresses herself with a certain elegance. "We want to observe the marriage ritual of the Fulani culture. These poor women are victims, oppressed, bullied by their traditions. It has to be exposed!"

Nafi, still smiling, speaks to the couple graciously, "Ah, so just like that, you're here to expose, to make your observations and expand the register of Western knowledge. We others, because of the constant concern for the common interest, we continue to be the objects of your observations. When will the agents change? Do you know the Africans who've gone to do observational, anthropological fieldwork on Westerners, particularly in your country, the United States? Some years ago, some very courageous African anthropologists trained in France decided to compare Malian sorcery to sorcery in Brittany. What a scandal those Malians provoked in France! Sure, we fill your universities and now, with the economic and political crises invading our countries, we stay there to work. I myself came back to this village because I couldn't take living in your country anymore. Here we have our peace and quiet with our daily problems."

Nafi knows how to talk to others. She keeps a light smile playing across her lips. Nafi isn't aggressive like Sula. She continues to speak, and we all listen. "I lived in your country for a long time, so I think I know it well. A pretty little vicious circle, on every level. In every field, we're represented by the titles and labels you assign us. It's useless to ask our opinion because we don't have one and we never will, such remains our condition. Humanity has to be liberated, doesn't it?" Nafi raises both arms to the sky, and without raising her voice, she continues to articulate these embarrassing reflections. "The Fulani, yet another effort to saturate the Western registers. Violence is a mundane subject. Those who suffer it can talk about it. But who will listen to them? These are the moments when repetition becomes the suspense of history.

"Sure, you denounce, but respect for the beliefs of others also counts. It's easy to trot out the discourse on culture, but it doesn't matter: the clichés are always there when you need them. The oppression of women is certainly a determining subject for you so-called liberated Western women. You've inscribed the rights and liberties of men in some sacred charter. Following that line of thought, you respect those rights and liberties, and so you have to spread them to protect those deprived of them. But what you refuse to understand, or what you understand very well, in all the irony of this fable, is that Fulani women remain what they are. Their desperate silence participates only in the vague symbols you create, which suffocate you and betray your guilt. In their obliviousness, they fight as they see fit, and that's all. Because you're the ones who still have the right to speak, even here, in their country. So, long live dependence! We play our cards according to your wishes, no problem."

Despite the fact that I absolutely must infiltrate the bouiboui, Nafi and Sula don't stop talking.

Without a change in tone, Nafi turns to Kate and says, "Okay, we'll work together from now on. We'll stick to you." Then Nafi adds this remark whose meaning escapes me completely: "And in any case, it's clear that once the loss has been recorded, a retreat into deep narcissism becomes the only inner resource. I invest my libido in Ada, and now in the search for this Affi."

Sula and Nafi withdraw to consult with each other.

And Ada, plunged back into her thoughts, tries to take stock of the situation.

Let the tam-tam drums awaken the ancestors, for nothing will stop Ada in her mission. All that remains is her loudly beating heart and her perpetual silence. Sula and Nafi return, hand in hand. The energy radiating from them is enough to move mountains. They aren't afraid of anything; they are made of life itself. It's truly a wonder to observe them. They speak in turn, like in church, in tones of apotheosis.

This time it's Sula who speaks to the young anthropologist couple: "You're going to introduce Ada into the Garba boui-boui by presenting her as your assistant. After all, you understand racial integration very well, and politically, your discourse is fashionable right now—it's impossible to disguise it, the breach has been struck. Sure, the United States, a country which calls itself democratic, a defender of the rights of man, hasn't yet resolved the question of the survival of certain races. Disparity hangs on the door to freedom along with all the other contradictions ensuing from these grand ideas. If only Blacks, dancing and singing as they do, could also lend their ears to the cruelty of their existence sung with resignation and grandeur by those who have rebelled. Then maybe they too would rebel in turn. Despite the violence that the rhythm of rap music inflicts on the ear, some songs are really quite incisive. I'm thinking particularly of the album *The Iceberg* by the L.A. rapper Ice-T who sings with so much hate and rebellion for the cause of American Blacks."

Sula continues her speech that oscillates between retreat and the affirmation of her ideas, displaying the elegance of her knowledge. She turns to Steve and asks him if he likes

Ice-T. A little intimidated, Steve responds with a barely audible no.

"That's okay," Sula says and vibrantly continues her complicated discussion of American popular culture. "So as I was saying . . . Ice-T reminds us no doubt that this form of capitalism instilled in the youth in the streets today, this mentality that the ends justify the means, isn't happening and never will. So let's just sleep peacefully. This idea is quite elementary, but à propos here. Of course this super power and its international integrity are problematic. But who would really dare to attack it resolutely, since it runs the world? The example of the Gulf War can only make us shudder. Its decline, dressed up in the ideology of the American dream, lives on in the imaginary with the rest of daily life. That nation, as developed as it is, still keeps its Blacks under its thumb, still takes from them the one thing that's worthwhile: the mind, as Ice-T so aptly says in one of his songs. That little weapon, none other than my conscience, my intelligence."

◆◇◆

"The turn toward simplicity expresses our current mood. Even if the entire system bewitches us into a stage of indefinition, keeps us in a stage of complete illusion, you will never lay a finger on my intelligence—the site of my power, my atomic bomb. Your TV screens are always showing Blacks at their worst moments. The Black drug addict, murderer, rapist. And as for the Black woman, she's an AIDS-ridden prostitute, a maid lost in the big dining room of a rich man who, seduced by her beauty and exoticism, doesn't think twice before fondling her backside as soon as the opportunity presents itself. In any case, she can be fired as soon as the boss loses interest in the roundness of her buttocks. She's on welfare, and let's not forget to mention the four snot-nosed kids hanging on her apron strings. But at the same time, the screens also insist upon the other side of the issue: indeed, there are Blacks with the illusion of having inserted themselves into a rigorous hierarchy where the petite bourgeoisie, or what we now call the nouveau riche, blends in. Like that General Colin L. Powell who, during the Gulf War, created a sensation all over the world. People admired him: a handsome Black man dressed in a military uniform weighted down with all those medals that mean nothing to us, but are adorned with so many honors in his own eyes. The good thing about the land of Bill—Bill Clinton, of course—is that it's impossible to place yourself outside of social realities. (He's the only president in the world who goes by Bill.) The journalists hammer this point home every time Powell himself starts to believe he's a man of genius, the status constructed for him by the media. He's Black in a white society, and he succeeded in becoming the head of the army of a world power! What a feat! What impossible beauty, what impossible misfortune. Even his ancestors from the islands would be impressed. Here is the heart of human problems—everything that isn't contradictory is false.

"They're certainly right to call him 'Oreo' because that dry cookie has a layer of white vanilla in the middle and is black as coal outside. (Those little cookies are really good. The combination of black and white melts on your tongue, slowly, leaving the taste of bitter and sweet, impossible to explain. You have to taste them yourself to have this indescribable experience.) In other words, only his skin is black, for he thinks like a person, that is, a white. For the record and in no particular order, let's cite those few names that resound violently but also sweetly in our ears, impelling us to forget all the human misery haunting the New York city streets: Eddie Murphy, Spike Lee, Oprah Winfrey, Denzel Washington, Miles Davis, and my favorite, Whoopi Goldberg—whose eyes cry out with joie de vivre—and plenty of others, of course. The list is rather long now at the end of the century. There's not one among them who doesn't have, from time to time, a guilty conscience for their part in this whole illusion of success. The list of names on the register of 'The Ones Who Made It' is rather phenomenal, they'd no doubt whisper in my ears plugged up from bad hygiene. But after how much time, I'd have to say, after how many centuries? It's certainly not a question of space or time. And yet the deep meanings of the Blacks' limping entry into the culture can mislead our thinking: the list of entries is growing at a speed that escapes us, as fast as the smoke of a cigarette smoked hastily in the cold of those winters that are impossible for the human body to bear." Sula has emptied her bag of pain onto this couple, as if she had been waiting for their arrival to get it out of her system.

◆◇◆

The role of black American lackey that Ada will assume shows quite plainly how social hierarchies function. The complexity of being double, of playing the authentic game of the relationship between dominant and dominated, allows them to reproduce the simulacrum.

A familiar tune. Nothing new there. Sula is now expressing herself with great sadness. She asserts herself in a monologue. Poor Ada listens to everyone without saying a word; only her internal reflections comfort her. She must do everything possible to ensure that Affi is still alive and to give her the hope that Siliki placed on her lips. Disguise herself as a Black American—a rather difficult task for her, even if it would be easy for Sula and Nafi. They know American culture well and will help Ada manage it. Sula is still talking while Nafi smiles. Steve and Kate seem worried and are giving off bad energy.

The more the girls talk, the more tension weighs down the atmosphere and the more the mystery of the situation sets in. Just at the moment when I think we will finally go our separate ways, Sula gently takes Kate's hand to feel the heat of her sweating skin. She keeps talking and talking. Sula won't release her prey for anything—she's worse than an iron maiden—but her speech is on the brink of despair. Then suddenly Sula's tone softens a little, like a child who wants to tell its mother something. Her voice enfolds itself in a shroud of sadness, a contagious kind of sadness. She keeps talking, but so slowly that she captures everyone's attention. Her eyes emit the same sadness as her words.

"You just have to juggle your cards right: what's inside stays there, and what's outside returns, provided it corresponds with the trend in exceptions. In America you can change your skin if you've got green bills, you can design your body according to the market. *Long live Jacko! Bonjour Jacko, I miss you! I haven't seen you since I've been back in Africa—I don't have a TV!* And the assortment of chemical products to straighten your hair is limitless, so you can resemble and reproduce the beauty norm determined by that classic standard: the white woman. Why straighten your hair? Perhaps to question endlessly is to share in all this modern madness, because it troubles us so much. The metaphor of the body is still only a detail. It's obvious that all of this gets under my skin. All I want to do is to find Affi, to help Ada. Solidarity, fraternity, liberty, love . . ."

Now Sula doesn't seem so agitated. We listen without interrupting her. Nafi and the young couple barely understand all the references in her speech. As for Ada, she is far from entering into this discourse—none of the references means anything to her. For her, this type of theatre is a mystery!

◆◇◆

"A physical disguise doesn't have any real consequences. The mask must always be worn. In short, these villagers are incapable of grasping the subtleties of the kind of thought we're dealing with here. It's not easy to demonstrate the depth of the questions at play in our world today. So what's the use then?" Sula laments brusquely. Ada's identity resists this flux and reflux of ideas imposed by the norm of a culture like the American one Sula and Nafi are talking about.

These anthropologists, who quite frankly interest absolutely no one, consult each other on the authenticity of their ideas and the moral value of their culture. Their goal is surely to live for something that extends beyond morality. Kate and Steve had not foreseen this chapter of their research in Africa. They know they should be ready for anything, but these two women have completely bombarded them. It's incredible how life can surprise you. While Kate and Steve talk about their helplessness and confusion, Ada plunges into the intimate thoughts that are slowly invading her. She is a jumble of emotions. She can't stop thinking about Affi and Siliki, her present occupation. Always in her thoughts, these two women appear to her under very different skies. They switch places in her mind: one of them appears clearly on the bluish background of her memories, the other appears as a shadow whose form she cannot completely distinguish. Ada can precisely remember the poignant look lighting up Affi's sad face. She recalls, too, her long neck, her fine plump lips in the outline of a sweet kiss, and other details too painful to evoke.

Someone brushes her shoulder—Kate, the anthropologist's wife. "We've decided to help you. But we refuse to take any responsibility if something goes wrong. So we need you to sign this form."

Sula, who has been following the scene, swoops in and grabs the paper from Kate's hand. Now when Sula talks, her voice holds so much anger that it practically trembles, as if she were about to suffocate. "Always on the side of power. I know that tune. How can you stay immune to what is happening to humanity? Hyperindustrialized Westerners act toward the rest of humanity as if they were supermen who have abandoned the savage and primitive mode of representing power or accessing the place of power. When they claim a humanity different from so-called underdeveloped groups who are the object of industrialized pity, it just sends me to the depths of despair." And she starts to cry softly. Nafi and I start to giggle nervously at the way Sula has let herself be carried away by her emotions, like a lost child trying to find its mother. Yet after this verbal release, Sula, now immobilized by despair, still has to sign the document. Nafi smiles, this time sardonically, because she feels the same pain. Gripped by anger, she cannot believe we must once more accept our usual fate in silence. "How awful! You reek! You reek like your stinking ideas!"

Sula and Nafi scream out their anger. Ada is bleeding on the inside. All her wounds are bleeding again. This scene has definitively driven home the world's blades once and for all. Then Nafi regains her calm enough to talk again softly, as if she were whispering in someone's ear.

"I refuse to believe that you're my enemies because for me, the enemy is the totality of all the mechanisms that debase the other. Unbelievable! Nothing came out of all this gray matter that we've just used so determinedly to explain our manner of conceiving the world to you. Even with all the elegance of our knowledge, we didn't manage it. One more time we've just been preaching in the desert." Nafi looks Kate right in the eye and explains, "No, no, you won't get any signature. Ada won't sign anything, and she'll stick to you regardless. Nothing will go wrong, I guarantee you. Me, Nafi, the girl who swears on her Fulani ancestors."

Not reassured, Kate calls her husband to negotiate the situation with these girls. As soon as he approaches, Nafi snatches the document from his hands and tears it into a thousand pieces. There. Satisfied.

As Nafi talks, she gestures for the couple to listen. "Open your ears now to the muffled voices in your representation of the world. The document is no more, and let's not discuss it any further." She explains to Steve that it's completely useless to insist on legal responsibilities or other such garbage because we have no intention of signing anything whatsoever and anyway, they don't have any choice about accepting Ada as either their assistant or their housekeeper traveling with them.

Sula and Nafi lose a lot of time on all these useless negotiations. They aren't asking for the impossible; they simply want Ada infiltrated into the boui-boui. Americans have the possibility of spending time observing the girls shut up there, and perhaps of approaching them, talking to them, touching them if need be.

Surprised by Sula and Nafi's imposing, authoritative outbursts, Steve and Kate are struck dumb for several moments. Shock. They can't believe what is happening to them in this Fulani village. Finding two women who have lived in their country and now besiege them with all sorts of received ideas about the United States—it's incredible. Plus it's so hot that flies are starting to infest the place, and the station is heaving with people.

Finally, Kate and Steve invite Sula, Nafi, and Ada to their hotel for the evening. Delighted by this decision, Nafi, Sula, and Ada follow them, humming a melody, sad but sweet.

Sula is beaming with joy and explains to Ada that they've just accomplished something more for their history of forgotten women in the village. Despite their aggressiveness, they remain effective. They contribute to the cause of women. Sula and Nafi's eyes look happy, but with a layer of melancholy underneath. Kate, walking next to them, detects this air of sadness. Entire days pass without further negotiation. Sula and Nafi leave me with Kate and Steve after giving copious recommendations.

Ada stays by herself, so sad without the company of the others.

Sula and Nafi are amazing women. They both touch me deeply, each in her own way. Ada settles in with Kate and Steve in their hotel for several days, and she finally asks them to fix an appointment to start their research at the boui-boui. They don't seem to be in any rush. They spend all their time taking long walks in the village, reading, swimming. Ada clearly has no room in her life right now for all of these supposedly mind-enriching activities. Her own mind is instead weighed down by the all the twists and turns in the life of a woman in these far-flung villages. She is quite frankly losing patience. She feels like a prisoner again, like in her Baba's household. Nothing ever seems to change in her life. Sometimes Ada feels like their slave. She has to stay pent up in the hotel while they read, and go swimming when they swim. In short, Ada has to do such violence to herself to keep from flaring up at them as they pursue these idle activities. But she mustn't get lost in despair. She must become familiar with the whole process of confinement, its meaning and purpose. As the days pass, Ada thinks of Affi: maybe she's already at her husband's house? And if that's the case, how will she find her abode?

◆◇◆

Calm reigns in the village, as usual. Under the big trees, mats are laid out, arranged in groups of four or six, and occupied by entire families exhausted by the heat and their work in the fields. From time to time, traditional music, playing somewhere in the background, rocks them gently in their light afternoon sleep. At the end of the afternoon, nature's bright colors proclaim themselves in a tinted blend on the canvas of the sky, between the setting sun and the moon slowly climbing the horizon. The darkness of the night is fearsome, and for good reason: you can't help but imagine that it conceals murders and other shady deeds practiced only in the depths of darkness. Two weeks have passed since Steve and Kate's arrival in the village. Imagine, for just a moment, the joy Ada feels when they ask her to go with them to make an appointment for their first visit to the Garba boui-boui. Now she must go over all the preparations. But Ada is so excited by the idea of finally having Affi before her that she panics a little. She's sure to forget the important details, to forget to keep quiet and let Steve and Kate do the talking. The day's plan of action is to disguise herself appropriately for this first occasion. Calm, calm, self-mastery, Ada whispers to herself in the depths of her heart, which seems to have rediscovered happiness. She dashes into her room and begins to put together her disguise. They need to be there before nightfall. Ada runs through the final details, taking the time to prepare herself morally and physically. It would be impossible to drop in on Sula and Nafi.

But back in her room, she collapses on the bed, crying so hard that her tears strangle her, like they used to. In her mind, she sees all the unexpected events in her life these past years. Someone knocks on her door so violently that she leaps out of bed as if snapping out of a nightmare. Kate simply wants to make sure that Ada is getting ready. Outside there is a crushing heat like at the start of every afternoon, so stifling that as soon as you lie down on a bed, sleep snatches you away.

"We leave in fifteen minutes, if that's ok." Ada quickly washes her oily, sleepy face, brushes her hair back, and slips on an utterly American cap bearing the words "Game Boy" that Steve gave her one day when they were walking under the burning sun. Slowly, she makes up her face, whistling all the while. Her hands fumble a little, but she manages to make herself up delicately in lively colors. While maintaining a certain simplicity, she still succeeds in breaking out of the ordinary. She puts on a simple skirt with a tight-fitting T-shirt that accentuates the roundness of her large breasts. She has white tennis shoes on her feet paired with strangely patterned white socks, a gift from Kate. Ada is done up like an American, a real African American straight out of Harlem. Steve and Kate are dressed in shorts and T-shirts paired with shabby tennis shoes and socks of impeccable whiteness, looking like the Americans you find on every street and boulevard in the United States.

A guide is waiting for them at the hotel exit. It's the middle of the afternoon, and the village is regaining the rhythm of a place that is actually inhabited. Children are goofing around in every corner of the village. As soon as they see us passing by, they stop and stare until we disappear from view. Some follow us, so the guide turns around and says something inaudible as he taps into his hand. In the distance, you can see the backs of women bent down at work. We walk in the serenity of the village. Ada's heart is beating hard, but she doesn't tremble because her soul is at peace as she advances. She recognizes the boui-boui from afar. Now, she can appreciate the beauty of the place. The Garba boui-boui is encircled by tall ferns and other great flowering trees. The carefully cut lawn at the entrance gives the impression of a dignitary's property. One of the caretakers welcomes us with a big smile and endless greetings. From behind, Kate and Ada listen to Steve explain to the caretaker that we intend to begin our observations. Indeed, Ada uses the designation *we* in her mind, for she believes she has succeeded at the first steps of her infiltration into the Garba boui-boui.

While Steve converses with the caretaker, her memory gives itself over to all sorts of imaginary reconstitutions. Somehow or other she will discover what is hiding in the boui-boui. She is so restless with victory that her imagination blooms, as if in a tender night where her cry of hope had been suffocating. Ada imagines being transformed into a big black rat tickling Affi's toes. And if only she could be a flea, she would slip into Affi's left armpit and give her tiny little love bites, just to reawaken her sleeping senses. She would do the impossible to find the pretty Kallima butterfly, a colorful species from Java. It would land right on her nose, leaving a pinch of rose pollen. Steve sets the first appointment for two days later. To make sure she has it right, Ada repeats the date in her head: two days after today's date. As we leave, we shake the caretaker's hand and introduce ourselves in turn, like in grand decoration ceremonies for some sort of honor. She is cold, no doubt hardened by the inhumane work that she has been practicing for so long.

Steve and Kate leave early the next morning to visit the neighboring village behind the hills. There, the women are completely nude; they don't even wear a cache-sexe. The men don't allow them to wear clothing: clothes, they think, are a sign of superiority. Women must leave that privilege to men. People are attracted to the village to see these naked women and satisfy their fantasies, but also quite simply to get an eyeful of beauty. It seems that these women's bare torsos are often covered with infinitely varied tattoos that suggest, with the harmony of their lines, a certain artistic sensibility. They might be compared to the intricate black lace that old ladies knot and loop for days on end. They might also call to mind leatherwork whose delicate surface slides under the touch of a hand. One hardly dares to imagine the ridicule in the glances of people like Kate and Steve there.

◆◇◆

Ada spends the day alone, imagining all kinds of possibilities for getting Affi out of the boui-boui. She returns to its surroundings to study the place. While she hovers there, she discovers the backwater where the girls wash at nightfall. It's impossible to see someone's face at night without the help of light. Ada is not interested in admiring the girls' silhouettes and excludes that possibility from her projects. Ada hangs around the boui-boui so long that she becomes sick of it. With feeble steps, she returns to the hotel and lets the cold water run over her head as she reflects on all these events. She had found it impossible to eat during the day, and anyway, she's still not hungry. Like a little bird, she returns to her nest of solitude, her head empty of all reminiscence, of all wild wandering. She lies down and no doubt sleeps deeply.

In the middle of the afternoon the next day there is an unbearable commotion and menacing heat. It's one of the hottest times of the day, and the heat beats down violently. From afar, she hears voices and noises that finally wrest her from her sleep. Amidst the cries and tears, panic replaces the village's habitual calm. In one bound, she jumps from the bed, wraps herself in a pagne lying on the floor and leaves the room in another bound. Everyone is yelling at once, and she can't make out what is being said in all the chaos. Made desperate by the tumult of voices and with an arrogance that surprises even herself, she grips a woman and shouts into her ear, "What's going on?"

"Hé! You don't know?"

"No! What . . ."

"The Garba boui-boui is burning. It seems some of the girls will perish in the fire."

Without waiting for her to finish, Ada begins to hop like a grasshopper. Shoeless, bare-breasted, she fixes her pagne tightly around her hips and in a burst of momentum, runs along the track to reach the boui-boui. She feels the track roiling under her feet from the torrid heat, but she can't stop. The wind of misfortune is pushing her on, and she feels light, despite the enormous difficulty of running without a bra, given the cumbersome chest that her burdens her little body.

A hurly-burly of cries and furious voices rises up as she approaches the crowd, a confusion of shouts and strident wailing, of appeals and pleading that grows into a caco-phony. The noise plunges her back into the same nightmare that constitutes the drama of her life. In just a short instant, it's all over. The boui-boui is no more. The smoke chokes the crowd of people gathered there.

As soon as Steve and Kate see Ada, they come over to her. She is crying, tears covering her face. Kate speaks gently, "I'm sorry, Ada." Her eyes, so blue among the other eyes, unsettle Ada momentarily. Disconcerted, she casts her gaze aside. In the distance, she sees a piece of the embroidered mat that belonged to Affi floating in the smoke. Here and there bits of paper hover in the ashes. Ada gathers a few, you never know, she might find fragments of Affi's intimate journal which would reveal the history of her mother Siliki. Here and now, in her agony of no return, she feels more intensely than ever Siliki's tenderness and generosity. The movement of her thoughts follows that of her body as she tries to capture the flying bits of paper, when suddenly her right foot strikes a hot stone. Underneath, she finds a little notebook that she slips under her armpit. It is still warm and covered with ashes. Ada fastens onto this object like a child clutching her mother's skirt. She shivers and leaves this cursed place. She seeks a refuge where she can savor the journal, and she heads toward the still pool that reminds her of Siliki's dear backwater in Mafa country. Now, instead, she is at the Fulani country backwater where Affi used to wash, sometimes at dawn, sometimes late in the evening. The atmosphere is so serene as afternoon comes to a close that she stays there, calmly looking into space. A light breeze blows and she can hear the sound of the leaves tossed every which way. With a heavy heart, Ada advances gently into the void, where all her memories are jumbled and muddled up and only the image of Siliki appears clearly. The presence of this powerful image stirs vapors of tenderness in Ada. She finds a rock to settle down on and begins to read the notebook which, to her great surprise, belonged to Affi. The details of the fire and all the rest don't interest her anymore, for a door has been closed, leaving a great commotion in her head, and this clamor, which she alone can understand, will resonate in the shadows. It is closure, once and for all.

Ada's great joy, if she has one, is to throw up a smoke-screen to anyone trying to enter her life. Like a flying fish caught in turbulent waves, she often emerges in unexpected places. Her two brothers, who had accompanied her the first time she had decided to seek the Garba boui-boui, will never know that she returned there all alone. As if it were yesterday, she sees her brother's reaction when he had spied Siliki lying on the ground. He leapt away at the approach of her rags, which seized his throat with their usual nauseating smell. Her brother, aside from those odors which have been burned into his sense of smell, will never know that Siliki had a daughter or that it was for this daughter that Ada found herself in this village again. Risking her own life for the woman she loves is only a small proof of her love. Her brothers love her imagination; for Ada, they're ready to launch an assault on the summits.

Opening the little ash-covered notebook, without skipping a line or leaving out a word, Ada reads the following passage; now it alone speaks to her imagination: *She was thrown into a well full of caimans, who devoured her legs . . . As for me, show reverence for all the ashes that rise into the air. How beautiful it is to quit this world and leave behind only ashes! My ashes will fly to unknown lands, carried by the unpredictable wind.*

The sun sets slowly as the moon climbs the hills, all under her grim gaze, while in her soul she thinks how only women know how to make her live, in the shadows and in the lights; they alone, in their lives, so full and complex, seduce Ada. And they alone, in their elusive wanderings, know how to give her a place in their hearts

Ada whispers to herself, this time words of kindness. In the other world, she will not say that she has suffered because she received so much love from Siliki. In the present world, only the absence of love rattles her soul and casts her into the shadows.

PORTRAIT OF A YOUNG ARTISTE FROM BONA MBELLA

To my mother, Augustine Naniama

Life is short, but boredom makes it longer.

—Jules Renard

Man's greatest act of cowardice is to keep silent. It is therefore incumbent upon everyone to speak aloud. It is my wish that this play will create a shockwave from within the great white silence of ideas.

—Sony Labou Tansi

OUR QUAT

> There isn't a single patch of earth inhabited
> by man where misery and misfortune haven't
> found a place for themselves.
>
> —*Tchicaya U Tam'si*

Standing on the corner of Rue de la Joie, I see my youth pass by. I still don't understand the need, when memories assail us, to return to this origin. But there it is: in my mind, the image of a friend asserts itself; little by little her silhouette becomes clearer. She's right beside me the instant I call her to mind. "I came back to the quat," I tell her. "Our street is more boisterous than ever, our neighborhood, the most glaring of all the quats in the city of Bona Mbella." That's how I speak to Miss Bami in my dreams. In my head, I can still hear her voice reasoning, opening a searing breach in time: "Chantou, I'm bored as usual. I'm so tired of this quat that I only think about one thing: leaving. I mean leaving far, far away and never coming back to this hole. Chantou, tell me something interesting. What are we going to do today? Ah! *We share the same appetites, we endure the same afflictions.* Hey, do you know who that quote is from?" Muriel Barbery. Come on! Of course, how would I have known? Books are rare here; I know that very well since all my father talks about is books. Every cent goes toward buying them. As soon as he finishes one, he boasts as if he had written it himself.

Miss Bami had a quick wit and an easy way with words. One day she told me a story she embellished at her leisure, a story I don't remember very well except that she concluded it with the sentence: *One must know how to separate the wheat from the chaff.* At that, I gave her the look of an accomplished cynic.

Miss Bami tackled questions—of whatever nature—with all seriousness. She couldn't end a tale without adorning it with a few clichés. I don't know what ever became of her. I'd like to see her someplace other than the whirring film reel of my memory, even if it's just to tell her that her cut-and-dried expressions don't impress me anymore. Good old Miss Bami! At the age of seventeen, I already found her eccentric.

I was born in Bona Mbella, an awful neighborhood, a world apart. I left it upon the death of a very dear friend. And I exiled myself to my father's library. I'd obtained a copy of the keys without him knowing it. I slipped into the room to filch magic books warped by the humidity. Poor man! He'd purchased a bulb whose radiation, he'd been assured, would help conserve them. But he was forced to watch his books crumble year after year, smelling of mildew. That failure gave him such grief. He missed his life in Europe: over there, at least, books didn't turn green with mold.

Already as a little child, I found myself surrounded by books. A hallowed feeling would seize hold of me when I discovered words of love that my father had scattered throughout the pages. They were intended for us, his children. Sometimes I happened across old photographs.

My father was as unusual as Miss Bami. A dandy, as they say! He collected young women; their photos—varied and multicolored—form part of my heritage. Sometimes I would discover a shot of my mother in the pile. She had her head shaved, her favorite hairstyle. Mama never wore a wig, never straightened her hair. She conjugated naturalness. I thought she looked exquisite like that. Of course, she's my mother—I wouldn't be capable of saying otherwise. Our parents can only be strong and beautiful; they're untouchable.

I adore my father, my flame. I won't recount our history—it belongs to us. He taught me to read banned books, banned at least for people in our neighborhood. I see us on a train. There's a young man in the same car, absorbed with a volume as greenish as the ones in my father's library. Papa livens up as soon as he sees a reader in his vicinity. A change comes over him; a smile brightens his face. He turns toward the young man: "What author are you reading, my son? Can I have a look at your book?" To the addressee's great surprise, my father snatches his book, only to realize that he is holding just half of Jean-Paul Sartre's *Words.* "My son, what happened to your book?"

"Papa, I don't know. My classmate lent it to me that way."

"In that case, give me your address. I'll send you a brand-new copy! You'll see how astounding it is in its entirety." My father missed his true calling as a bookseller!

Before he granted me entry to his library, he used to leave a few books in my room. Once I became an adult, I devoured them all, especially after his death when I moved them to my house, where they've been ever since. When I think of him, I sniff the pages, inhale the musty paper, take a volume off the shelf, touch it. When I do, I see my father, explaining the importance of such and such a book: "You should read instead of walking all the time!" Fortunately, Papa preserved that little corner. In withdrawing from the real world, I entered that one . . . Yes, me, Miss Bami's friend . . .

I'm saddened by the state of the neighborhood of my youth. I see the same scenes and images over and over, one after another like in a film where the heavy atmosphere makes your head swim. Whenever I think of it, my spirits fall. No words can reproduce those kinds of paintings: neither their former brilliance nor their current ugliness. I want to recreate the ambiance where I let myself be carried away by the rhythm of everyday voices. In spite of the imperatives of survival, the people still smiled, manifested a certain joie de vivre. The girls who aborted every year without it costing them their lives are an indication—a dreadful one, for sure— that we took advantage of our adolescence all the same. I'd like to embrace those times past where, dressed in dirty little knickers, we ate delicious corn *makala*. I remember how succulent they were, I'm nostalgic for them, yes, it gives me the blues . . . and in the end I sing to make them go away.

Growing up in Bona Mbella is no small affair. There people waver between joy and sadness, and eventually they get carried away by ecstasy. Sorrow slips into the interstices of all that we live. Like most children in the world, we're overexcited. We wander in the streets from morning till night, in search of events that will bring our young nerves to incandescence. I lose myself in reveries every time I fail to regain control of myself in this place. Each breath sends hot air into the face of your neighbor. Each gesture evokes the passage of time, recapturing the splendor and cruelty of a rite. Each image whirls once, twice, three times, thousands of times, like the torture wheel. Each smile opens the door to a far bluer sky. Each birth in Bona Mbella resolutely holds open the gaping hole from which blood continuously flows. Mothers are condemned to give life.

Bona Mbella is our People's China: acrid, torrid, life bubbling like spicy *pèpè* soup, spurting in every direction. The constant hubbub of the streets where sometimes a smell arises capable of turning your stomach. People of modest means roam around relentlessly, engaged in a common struggle: first, feed themselves; next, feed others, little ants stuffed into every nook and cranny of the quat. Looking for a bite to eat is a full-time occupation. They have to track down their daily bread. Nothing comes for free, everything has to be wrangled at a heavy price. Mothers suck their babies' little toes, and the infants cry despite the warm softness of their lips.

There's no clear line of demarcation between the rich and the poor in Bona Mbella. Everything is mixed up, except class consciousness. Sure, there are beggars, but in reality, poverty is everywhere.

In Bona Mbella, you can find anything, really anything! You only have to name your desire for some kid to satisfy it. The division of labor is clear cut. An invisible line delimits each person's territory and signals the job that must be done there. Having scruples is not a virtue. It's all about street smarts, a genius for *savoir-survivre*, knowing how to survive. The boys glue themselves to potential clients swarming the streets. The girls wait in sordid rooms where the smell of sperm and counterfeit virility hang in the air. How do those kids know you're looking for a rare object—a human bone, for example? How can they tell you're anxious to remain discreet? How do you negotiate an exchange of children, young girls, women? Who do you turn to in order to find a soothsayer or a renowned griotte? It matters very little what you're looking for: ask and you shall receive, seek and you shall find. Don't be afraid, keep trying is our motto. It haunts our imagination. Everything is transparent for those who really want something. The destitute understand that. Life grabs them by the guts. Nothing escapes them, except History, even if they breathe it, maybe without knowing it. Can you choose your fate? Your birthplace? It's always an accident.

Bona Mbella is the city's ghetto. But where is its truth? "The truth about a man lies first and foremost in what he hides," Malraux reminds us. But what can you really hide in our quat aside from shattered lives? To discover this place is a work of invention. How can you translate the Rue de la Joie's rhythm, its ambiance, its character? As that old woman says, Bona Mbella is deadly poetic. Whether it's a look, a smile, a gesture, a bit of hope, a brightly colored fabric . . . In spite of the mud, the stinking wells, the loitering children, the battered women, AIDS—they remain proud. Nobody's more full of themselves. Their energy comes straight from the source. The roots that bind them together are invisible and difficult to disentangle. When one rots, another sprouts. Here a death, there a birth.

Still, Bona Mbella produced the Decca family and its wildly rhythmed *makossa*. Who hasn't heard of Grace and Ben Decca? There's a third Decca whose first name escapes me, and maybe even a fourth singer. In any case, I only know the first two, Grace and Ben. They're called *Bana ba loko*, which means crowd warmers. They came out of the fringes of Bona Mbella. Just like her beautiful voice, Grace's behind—which people call "intelligent" and is shaped like the hinterland—has set more than a few people dreaming.

Jeans molded around her bottom, she wiggles in every direction when she walks. To the public, she's really something: swagger. You can hear the Deccas bawling out their songs on the international radio waves. From time to time, Ben also talks about Bona Mbella and his childhood. It's quite an achievement.

One mustn't forget, of course, the singer Douleur—the king of pop—and his divine voice. He doesn't wake the dead like Myriam Makeba does with her prophetic melodies. Douleur is reserved and timid but still manages to get his message across. Yes, he's another Bona Mbella Boy.

In the quat, music serves to soothe children who become true creators. They make their tam-tams reverberate, the drums singing of sweet pleasures to anguished souls. They muddle sounds, from makossa to zengué, from jazz to blues. They make their guitars screech . . . In the dark of night, the children of Bona Mbella draw rare vibrations from their instruments.

"*Tragedy begins here*," declares Nietzsche. *The Gay Science* (which I read with my father) is a book for everyone who lives in our space. Tragedy does begin here, in a bed where everything falls dramatically apart. The nights there are memorable—hot and sticky. Humid air infiltrates through half-open windows. Waking arrives with a certain feverishness. Dawn softens heartless souls. If the nights are unforgettable, the days display a disturbing and uncertain poetry. Among the droppings, sometimes you catch a bit of freshness. The tragic manifests itself when there is no more lyricism in the air.

One detail merits more attention: the thick fog that covers the Bona Mbella sky every evening. It diffuses a light whose energy permeates us. Thus descends the hour of storytellers. From time to time, one discerns a gleam of clarity in the shadows of the stories so passionately narrated. Authorship is inserted by ending the tale with: *it's my story; I underline that; on the other hand, I sign my name, etc.* A stamp of legitimacy that establishes one's authority. Events are thus engraved in our memories forever. Each more or less precise episode belongs to the repertoire of anecdotes that nourish the neighborhood. That's how spells are ascribed to certain places . . .

Analyzing Bona Mbella remains a dilemma for me. The film unfolds hour after hour, minute after minute, always to the same rhythm. It's the everyday monotony that leads me to describe the quat's climate as drab. Evidently it's only in Bona Mbella that there's a robbery every night, that the piercing cry of the proprietor attracts a panic-stricken crowd. Occasionally, the thieves are arrested and the populace lets loose. Amid the scuffle, everyone is convinced of their right to cast the first stone.

Our mothers serve equally well for all the children of the quat. They advise us, supervise us, feed us, but also punish us. Sometimes their punishments are unforgettable. They hit hard, really hard. As for our fathers, they're out of touch. They've lost themselves in the bars, in the smell of their beer. Their gazes are fixed by pain.

In Bona Mbella, from the crack of dawn, young girls are out wearing aggressively red lipstick to entice passersby. Calves arched over towering high heels, they totter over to the beds that await them. The sumptuous beauty of early evening gives way in the wee hours to stale-breathed silence. The will to seduce clients fades at first light.

Bona Mbella Girls never master their destinies. A curious fact: they're often constipated. They eat too many ground-nuts. Their teeth, striking in their whiteness, are always chomping on peanuts. They don't drink alcohol, coffee, or tea. They only drink soda water, a gassy drink that produces farts and belches. No need to describe the concert that escapes from their bodies. Bona Mbella Girls are all desperate, but not a single one breathes a word about it. The desire to talk about oneself, which haunts so many of the bourgeoisie, hardly torments them. They're waiting for a miracle to happen, a miracle capable of changing their fates. They're waiting for Godot. Day after day . . .

Overseas, if they should meet each other there, they recognize each other, signal to each other with their get-ups, their flirtations, their money, in short all the look-at-me signs characteristic of ardent girls. As soon as they encounter each other—at a party for example—they reconcile like reunited family. They snub their brothers and cousins, just to make them pay for the harassment they put up with in adolescence. Anyway, the girls say, the boys don't have any *jass*, *dos*, green "In-God-We-Trust" bills. They're eternally broke. Sure, they're often elegant, real *bana ba wonja*—free children—but ick, ick, ick!

Frankly, I'll be the one to tell you, there are even hotter topics! My cousin Munyengue Kongossa has already said it: in our day, the sine qua non remains fail-safe cunnilingus from *whitey*. It's more than guaranteed, one hundred percent refundable in case of failure. Munyengue Kongossa functions as our common mouthpiece, our spokeswoman. Taking a disliking to her is pointless, and incurring her wrath leads to enormous inconveniences. Among Bona Mbella girls, the password is: dixit Munyengue. She reports all the stories of other girls. Secrets—she has none. The other girls say bad things about her, criticize her, but when the occasion presents itself, they're no less delighted to hear her juicy information. Everyone knows that Munyengue Kongossa spends her time talking about what doesn't concern her. It's repugnant, but she acts as if she doesn't care. She acts tough. Nobody tells her anything anymore. As her name indicates, *Munyengue* means joie de vivre, and *Kongossa* gossip. In short, she's a young woman who adores scandal. A sorceress of gossip.

When she doesn't have any fresh stories to sink her teeth into, she recycles old ones. Like any self-respecting Bona Mbella Girl, she does it Bona-Mbella style. What I admire most about her is her savoir-faire for fresh detail. As unbelievable as it may seem, Munyengue Kongossa is Evil itself. Not only can our smooth talker fill an entire dossier about the person she's chosen to disparage, but her audience can also cover library shelves worth of pages. MK, as her friends call her, always enjoys herself immensely, and she knows that everybody takes pleasure in listening to her. The old women in the quat appreciate her gibes. You could do a case study on Munyengue Kongossa, who lives her life with exaggerated charm. Her speech is a slippery slope. Words fall into line as they come out of her mouth like from a perpetually leaky faucet. When she speaks, she hardly stops for breath. She pours out dirty stories the whole blessed day.

According to her, *whitey* loves *downtown* and visits there regularly. Defiantly, Munyengue Kongossa proposes that her best friend act on it.

"No thank you," retorts the other girl, "I don't like being licked like a dog."

"Oh, girly! How dull. Relax, little one. It's delightful, I promise you." Munyengue Kongossa is insistent and continues her presentation For *whitey*, cunnilingus exists for those who want to make use of it. Each visit downtown boosts his negotiations with incredible interest.

"No way," says the Bona Mbella Boy, "I refuse to visit the Netherlands—"

"You mean *downtown*," MK confidently corrects him.

"—I prefer *uptown*. My performance is more impressive there," he answers back. "Why ask the impossible? Downtown cunnilingus is not in my jurisdiction anymore."

"In that case, too bad for you. So it's for *whitey* to exclaim: Learn to live with the times! No realm should remain foreign to you. Always uptown, never downtown, but my dear Bona Mbella Boy, habits change!" The neighborhood boys are instantly downgraded.

MK asks her friend if the proposition still hasn't made her salivate. She murmurs in her ear, "Between us, I'd like to show you just how cunnilingus works. I adore those girls from Ngodi who strut all over the city. I'll tell you how they snub their cousins."

In Ngodi, there are five girls who've revealed they perform cunnilingus on other young women. Or at least girls who don't do "that" anymore with men, only women. Those girls, who shall remain nameless, make the rounds of the hottest nightspots in the city. Perched over beers, cigarettes between their lips, they're all smiles for anyone who'll buy them more beers, in sufficient quantity, that is, for an evening . . .

To hear them talk, the inhabitants of Ngodi are far from imagining the girls' sexual mores. For many a *showman* in the city, they're just hookers looking for clients, like those swarming the streets of Ngodi. A few *showmen* were so convinced of this that they put their foot in it by offering the girls a drink—in the secret hope of getting a free one. And that went on until tongues loosened enough to let the unbelievable slip: "Those girls you see over there are all lesbians. The one with the cell phone in her hand, that's their 'boyfriend.'" You started hearing that around Ngodi. More precisely, in the Bona Mbella nightspots, Sunday June 7 last. In one of the neighborhood discos, a group of young girls was dancing. Lost in a trance, they jiggled around and, intertwined, mimed the sex act in front of the dumbfounded young people. Thinking it was simply a matter of hookers out to get a lover for the night, one boy, clearly wasted, made a sign to one of the girls and engaged her in conversation. Not for long, poor guy. No sooner had he proposed "that" to his fleeting partner than the girl with the cell loomed up beside them like a fury: "No, she's not moving an inch! You've got to excuse me, but she's my woman, and I adore her!" At that, she lovingly wrapped herself around the other, not without letting fly a few salacious words: "My pleasure is at its height when I make love to her. It's over with boys! Basta! We're evolving!"

The brothers in Bona Mbella have it really hard. Life remains a constant struggle. They're not even worth talking about. Or even less crossing swords with. I don't know what soap the guys use, but they smell something awful. Plus they squeal like rats when they go after you. In short, a single piece of advice: avoid the boys in the quat.

Bona Mbella Girls are proud to play the role of exotic fruit at *whitey*'s side. Just imagine it! *Black is black, say it loud, I'm black and proud! Black is beautiful—yes, I'm black and proud!* Thank you, James Brown, you're still my idol! Reread Angela Davis, and don't forget the Black Power movement with Stokely Carmichael, Marcus Garvey, Malcolm X, Julius Lester and his book *Look Out, Whitey! Black Power's Gon' Get Your Mama!* We should think about taking another look at the slogans of the 60s. Today the word *nigger* doesn't mean anything. It's whiteness that counts, for men as well as women. You only have to read the literature from the African diaspora. It's useless to keep trotting out the history of colonialism. I'm thinking in particular of Daniel Biyaoula who calls attention to skin whitening in *The Impasse*. There are African countries where scrubbing off the epidermis has become a real source of commerce. They all cling to the OMO laundry soap ad that promised to wash whiter than white. Be whiter than *blanc*, more *blanc* than *whitey*—that's what's chic these days. In any case, we'll never forget you, Michael Jackson. You were only a product of your time. We love you with your whiteness. Unbelievable, but times are changing!

In Bona Mbella, the flesh trade grows a little more each day. Captivated by new technology and at the request of a perverse *whitey*, a girl from Bona Mbella sent the man a photo of herself naked. He then posted it on Yahoo, visited by people the world over. Her boyfriend, shocked by the image, then displayed it on all the telephone poles on NgoaKélé campus. Distraught beyond consolation, the victim took her own life. If only Bona Mbella Girls could understand that a *whitey* with decent morals is a pipe dream . . . How can you forget yourself to that point?

The cold war is at its peak. Whoever knows the Bona Mbella Boy knows that he never lets down his guard. Conscious of his power, he knows his sister will return to the fold: "*Whitey, whitey*, ok, but those people don't have any elegance! We're bursting with it . . . Our sisters aren't at risk of forgetting us. We've got a lot going for us. How will they manage? And what about memory?"

FIRST KISS

A breeze picks up, refreshing the air. I take a leisurely stroll through the quat.

Leaning against a post, two young girls are practicing the game of seduction: they're having a go at their first kiss. I contemplate them in silence. They kiss on the lips, touch each other, then draw closer. Titillated by the heat of their own bodies, their desire intensifies. They whisper *love mes, love yous*. A glow spreads across their faces, a glow of worry and joy. Time and space are theirs; nothing moves around them. The wind carries the echoes of their boldness, but they lack the experience of real lovers.

"Ow! You bit my lip! Don't you know how to kiss?"

I laugh quietly from my vantage point. I think back to my first smooch. Every time I place my lips on the mouth of a new conquest, I think of that day, and it still makes me shudder.

"Please, let me start again. Please. I promise I'll be careful. I won't bite you. I just wanted you to feel my love in the hollow of your lips, for the salt of your blood and saliva to mix in my mouth, for you to melt with joy from the bite, for the pain to make you crazy with love."

"Not a chance, you were useless! Stop talking nonsense! Learn to kiss instead of kicking up a fuss. Look! Your blabbering bruised my lips. Let them breathe a little . . ."

At the street corner, an intrepid Bona Mbella Boy is watching the huddled meeting of the two neophytes. They kiss once, twice, three more times, but there's no pleasure in it. What are you supposed to feel after a kiss? The Bona Mbella Boy is about the same age as the two girls swimming in saliva. Like a jealous animal, he leaps on one of them and gives her a long kiss. Once he's finished, he gives his clothes a shake of triumph. It's not that we have a difference of opinion; a man just can't stand for two young girls to kiss. "My friends will be proud of me when they hear about this," he says to himself.

Then he claps his hands, singing a Cameroonian soccer cheer, "We win, we win! *Zop-là, zop-là, zop-là!*"

"Mind your own business, you jerk! This is a lover's quarrel."

The girls get annoyed and start to pummel him. I don't intervene, just stroll on . . .

THE MOST BEAUTIFUL CALVES
IN THE WORLD

Would you believe that in Bona Mbella, calves interest us as much as anything else? The ones that look like Orangina bottles have always made me laugh. Or should I say Michelin calves. Judging by their admireuses' vote, they're the ones that always take the prize. Those Bibendum shapes (remember the Michelin mascot?), swollen in the middle but slender at the top and bottom, have such thin and charming "finales." Panè—a woman who's dead crazy about them—positively glows with happiness when she passes girls with Michelin calves. Who hasn't gazed at that plump little man on the tires of construction equipment? Look for him on all the brand's publicity. He's round all over except at the ankle and neck. Certain calves have the same constitution, no mistaking it. But when—who knows why—they suddenly start to look like beefcakes, then it gets serious. Our points of reference get confused. You can't tell their thighs from their calves—or their calves from their ankles, depending on how you look at it. Of course, in the eyes of Bibendum-calf aficionados, those known as beefcakes always walk away losers. No one looks at beefcakes, especially not Bona Mbella Boys. Girls with beefcakes always have a complex about them. But I find calves like that superb. I'd let my hands slide over them anytime.

Here's a pair coming toward us: it's the woman with the most beautiful calves in the world! The calves of a young lady in a miniskirt always fill me with the desire to caress them . . . Every one of her steps along the seaside tickles me. Are these feelings provoked by high heels? I don't know. Michelin calves are like statuettes: they're sturdy, built with strength. Their surfaces are like the face of the toughest tough guy.

Girls with beefcake calves, on the other hand, are of a singular sort. Beloved voyeuses, you who prefer Michelin calves, never forget that it's the smile that counts after all, that pure ivory smile to which your finest hesitations pitifully succumb.

THE MOVIE SCREEN

It's the weekend in Bona Mbella, and we're going around in circles in the quat. I want to go to the film club to see *Po di Sangui*, a movie by Flora Gomes, so I suggest to my friend Miss Bami a brief escape from our decaying neighborhood. Last week we saw Mweze Ngangura's *Pièces d'identité*. We loved one of the characters, Viva wa Viva: distinguished, very sure of himself, like most *sapeurs*, who have the devastating ability to impress the ladies—in short, a *Monsieur Gigolo*. He wears his clothes well, has cash to flash, goes from one woman to the next with the same sordid smile.

My best friend refuses to spend a franc. She says she's broke—like a lot of us, for that matter. We still manage to lay our hands on enough cash to go out to the movies, though. I think of Ma, who helps me out at times like these, but I'll keep myself from going to see her today. Between aunts, uncles, and various cousins—that is, endless family—there's always someone who'll come through for you. You just have to ask.

Despite the sometimes tedious gymnastics you have to go through, the money eventually emerges from a pocket or a chest, since Ma keeps her francs in her brassiere. As she pulls out the money, she reveals a hardened, dried-up breast. Her face clouds over, then fills with voluptuous tenderness. I'm so attached to her; I didn't have grandparents of my own. I love it when she caresses my head, kisses me on the mouth like Russians or South Africans do, or hugs me till my heart aches.

She makes me laugh, although she annoys her grand-daughters. True, I don't live with her. I only see her from time to time, which protects me from the deadliness of her incessant talking. Impossible to sleep, her descendant complains. If only she were struck dumb, even for a few hours, it would be wonderful!

After making the rounds, we've got enough to pay for tickets to the Rex in Akwa.

I ask my friend if we can use the opportunity to go to the film club and see the Gomes film again, and also the one by Jean-Pierre Bekolo, *Quartier Mozart*, with Saturday and My Guy.

"I hate African films! There's no action. Their main feature is how slow they are. I know you're going to tell me that that's their aesthetic . . ."

"Enough, Miss Bami, you're talking nonsense! Those films are excellent! They show how we live. You're not going to tell me that Saturday isn't an exceptional actress? Her accent, the way she works her body, her gestures . . . Of course, I can't figure her out."

"Oh come on, really, Chantou, I don't want to offend you, but I'd rather spend time in a different universe than the one I know so well. I live here, you know? Arid land, hunger, people howling all day long, not even to mention the rest of it. I don't need to go see that on screen, honestly! At the Rex, I find something that lets me leave the theater with a smile. The Indian dancers and their jewellery fire my imagination! There's always something about Bombay playing there."

India produces films that it distributes to African countries free of charge. Bollywood is popular in Africa now. Miss Bami's wild about it. She admires the dancers' hour-glass figures. She can see the same movie two, three, four, five times . . . Eventually she gets to know the names of all the actors by heart. She can tell you the exact moment when they'll come on screen, when the music starts, when it stops, who kills whom at which moment. Such a lovely little hell!

"Here's some more of your nonsense! You're forgetting that Nollywood exists now with a rare kind of repertoire. Honestly, you should keep your mouth closed now and then. Yeah, you're so annoying sometimes and ignorant most of all. Maybe you're not up to date, but Nollywood is outdoing itself, not only in Hollywood but also in Bollywood. Your little Indian dancers have been replaced by the buxom women of Ghana and Nigeria. I for one am thrilled to see all those calves and juicy lips, that nodding gait to the left, one, to the right, two, and hop, hop, and hop, hop. They float in a sensual ambiance that makes your head spin deliciously. From now on, it's a tie. Black light exists, and it's sumptuous."

Children who can't afford a ticket turn up at Miss Bami's place, which becomes a projection screen. Imitating the actors, faithfully reproducing their gestures, she gives the kids a hearty laugh. After each performance she tells them, "Tomorrow you'll pay me in kind!" Then she bursts out laughing herself, happy.

The children adore her. They're delighted to draw her some water, sweep her courtyard, or complete some little task.

With Miss Bami, the children don't suffer from loneliness, and they're constantly urged to excel. For my friend and the little ones around her, life reinvents itself daily.

"Hey, my dear Miss Bami, you missed the film of your life: *Waiting for Valdez* by Dumisani, a South African. It's a 25-minute short. I thought of you because it's the story of a kid who lives with his grandmother. He and his friends love the movies, but they're even more broke than we are. They all chip in so that one of them can go see the movie, and then he gives the others an unforgettable rendition! It's really great!"

"I had that idea before this director of yours, admit it! I've been playing the neighborhood movie screen for years! Imagination, my dear, imagination is learning to create when you lack the means!"

THE REVENANT

I'm welcoming a childhood friend. Like all Bona Mbella Girls who live abroad, my friend Munyengue Kongossa comes back to Bona Mbella for vacation. Before getting on the airplane, you've got to take care of your appearance, often starting with your hair. I solved the problem by shaving my head, but that wasn't the case for Munyengue Kongossa. She wants to mark the occasion, so her hairstyle will be as original as possible. For days she goes from one salon to the next to track down the ideal look. Which will she choose? She finally opts for a Mohawk, dyed blonde.

She hasn't gained an ounce. On the contrary, she's got killer arms. It's from all that weightlifting, poor girl! And now she's out to find some old friends.

She knocks at the Dikonguès'.

"Hello, mother. It's Munyengue Kongossa, Mbango's friend."

Mother Dikonguè slams the gate closed and starts shouting, "Come quick, there's a ghost at the door!"

Munyengue Kongossa narrows her eyes.

"Hey, what's the matter? I'm just looking for Mbango. I wanted to say hello. We haven't seen each other for a long time."

Father Dikonguè comes out to scrutinize the visitor.

"Who did you say you are, my girl?"

"Munyengue Kongossa, the daughter of Pa Munyengue, across from the water tower. I went to primary school and

Alfred Saker High School with Mbango, Bito, Miss Bami, and the other girls from the quat."

"Ah, but you look like a ghost, my girl! What kind of hairdo is that? Is it Mbenguè? You mean to tell me that in Paree, *la belle France*, people wear their hair like that? My daughter Mbango lives in Dole now. She married a boy from the Jura. They have two kids: a girl, Anaïs, and a boy, Hugo. I would have liked my grandchildren to have African names, but seeing as they're mixed and live over there, the white grandparents are the ones who get their way. Here we would have named the girl Sikè and the boy Ekambi. You haven't forgotten, have you, Kongossa? You're the one who advised my daughter to chase after *whitey*. Well, she found one on Bona Mbella beach."

"Could I have her address?"

"No, my girl, you'd frighten her with that hairdo. She's changed a lot, you know. She's taken up religion. She belongs to that sect, the Celestial Church of Christ. She never comes to visit, since we don't approve of her marriage or her religion."

"Fine, I'm out of here if that's how it is now."

"What about me, your old friend Chantou?"

"You never change, except that now you've managed to find a life partner, a woman you love and who loves you too. It's so strange that the people in the quat don't say anything about your sex life. Around here, everything goes unsaid. We don't feel anything!"

Munyengue Kongossa roams the neighborhood. No one wants to talk to her because, as they say, you should think everything that you say but not say everything that you think. Words get caught in her throat and erupt into belches.

She tries to pick fights left and right. Two days before her return to Europe, she gets attacked by street kids. She comes out of it with a broken arm, half her Mohawk missing, and a black eye.

I go to wish her goodbye. What a surprise to find her all banged up! Will she ever come back to Bona Mbella? Nothing's less certain.

"Hi, Chantou. How are you?" she greets me in that booming way of hers.

"Say, the boys in the quat really got you good. Were they out for your hide or what?"

"The quat has really changed," she replies. "Have all the old women who called me by name died? I really liked them—they used to listen to my stories! But I'm proud of you. You live your life, embrace your homosexuality. That's great . . ."

COUSIN KALATI'S TALE

Cousin Kalati is on vacation from Cuba. A cigar in her mouth, she pontificates, and in so doing, accurately recreates the situation prevailing in Bona Mbella. As her name *Kalati* indicates, she opens her book. A shadow directed at others. For example, on the subject of her aunt, her mother's sister, she says, "In her own way—which is brutal, like everything that happens there—Auntie, more than anyone, suffered from colonial violence. So many women were separated from their children who went to live in the West, never to see them again. It's tragic! Take Auntie: all her children left her one after the other. (Although I tend to forget Chantou, my dear scatterbrained cousin, the dyke who sucks girls' breasts. She's there, but she doesn't really count as a child of the family. Shhh, it's a secret.) It's the same with my mother as with Auntie. My father, returning from a walk, bluntly announced his departure. And then came my turn. In the meantime, when I was only ten years old, my mother remarried. My stepfather tore me from my auntie's skirts, like a mango that the wind hurls to the ground, at the risk of breaking it into a thousand pieces. I had to leave, quit Bona Mbella for France and attend a school in a nice neighborhood on the outskirts of Paris. Auntie cried so much that people told her, 'Listen, your niece isn't dead. She just went to live with the child-eaters, and she'll attend the best schools in the world!' It was no use. My departure was a day of mourning for Auntie, and she was in mourning until the day she died."

Chewing on her cigar, Cousin Kalati shakes her head and interrupts herself a moment, "An accident of birth. How can we change it? I live with my history, my past, and I construct the future. In the limbo of the Pacific, a map takes shape, circulates. The lines represent the network of ports of call through which our boat passed. My life is an archipelago of histories. I'll never know how to shift its curve . . ."

Cousin Kalati, the cigar now in her hand, now in her mouth, continues to talk about her aunt: "My auntie had a single worry: to feed us every day. I remember that she used to say to Auntie Ebègnè, her lover (shhh, that's confidential), 'If anything should ever happen to me, please do everything you can for my grandchildren!' The two friends would laugh, then say in chorus, 'Our grandchildren, of course! My grandchildren are also yours!'"

Cousin Kalati, cigar in her mouth, scans her audience and then continues: "Auntie Ebègnè didn't have any children of her own, and our family became hers. My auntie was poor, simple, rustic. My uncle met her in a neighboring village, where they were married. She served her husband and children without ever complaining: they were everything to her. When my uncle finished his studies in medicine, he left his wife. From that day on, Auntie was caught in the spiral of social violence. She acted as if nothing had happened. In her mind, my uncle, in a particularly vehement tone, continued to boss her around like a second-class maid. She complied without any resistance. For her, obedience was a duty. She was her husband's property. He claimed to have paid an incredible dowry for her. My auntie had a very soft voice, barely audible, and my grandfather liked that. He often said that he didn't like women who spoke too loudly. After the divorce, Auntie became talkative to the point of being tiresome. I can see her now (she laughed all the time) recounting her life with her childhood friends, whom she called 'the chatterboxes.'"

Cousin Kalati finishes the last sentence with a quick exclamation, takes a drag on her cigar, puffs the smoke out in rings, then continues: "My auntie knew everyone. She saw them being born, and then she saw them die. She knew each of them in detail. She could say who was kind, generous, approachable. And who was mean, ungrateful or underhanded. In short, she was the mistress of the neighborhood. 'Woe to those who came upon those good women who were always shooting their mouths off,' Auntie would roar. 'However much you beat them, they never felt a thing. On the contrary, the blows only made things worse, which sharpened their tongues. So they came out with even more monstrous bits of foolishness!'"

Cousin Kalati elegantly twists the corner of her lower lip with her tongue sticking out and the cigar between the fingers of her left hand. She rolls her eyes, a different tone to her voice. "My uncle is a little man, very elegant, with a cold, dull gaze. On his forehead, a furrow of wrinkles forms the lines of a tragic history. Sharp-witted with honest eyes, he's an incorruptible employee of the hospital where he practices. He's the last representative of that *belle époque*, the sixties. I didn't know him, but I confess I probably wouldn't have liked him very much. He was a superior sort of soul. I have a photo of him. He's wearing a sharp black suit, a bowler hat, polished shoes. People always complimented my grandmother on her husband's elegance."

Cousin Kalati sits up straight in her chair and squeezes the cigar between her lips, making a strange noise. But her words are still on her side. "For my auntie, the postcolony began and ended at the Douala airport, where she saw each of her children fly off on an airplane that would take them west. Those who could came back after a few years, then left again just as quickly. The situation in the country not being favorable to new ideas, they went into exile for good. There were others who, once they left for the airport, never returned to have their hair caressed by Auntie. 'All this hullabaloo started with my husband, who ran off to the Whites,' she used to say. Along with Auntie Ebègnè, her life companion, she was never able to pronounce that terrible name: France. Instead, they always said *Mbenguè bakala*, in Duala, '*the country of the Whites*,' which also implies 'the country that stole our children from us.'"

Cousin Kalati still doesn't leave off her cigar, which goes from her mouth to her hands. "It's curious," she says, "Auntie couldn't imagine what the West represented for her children. She only knew that they had left her without any hope of return. For her, the *mukala* was a person who ate children at night and during the day went about their business, with a yellowed smile and a fresh-smelling, handsome suit. My auntie hated that race of child-eaters. If she suffered so much to see her children surrender to the temptation of the West, it's easy to imagine that other mothers did as well. They never saw their children again as long as they lived. Those children settled abroad and then didn't budge. My auntie, along with many others, was a mother who had lost her children. People called them the eternal weepers, the same as the *madres del cinco de Mayo* in Argentina, or Rachel who cries for her children in the Holy Bible. 'All this misfortune comes from a history that has joined us to the Whites forever . . .' confided that steadfast woman."

Cousin Kalati gets up, pensive, focused, left hand on her hip, cigar in her right, a smile on her lips. It's silly, but Cousin Kalati and her stories have seriously gotten on my nerves. I want to open the breach onto new stories.

THE MUTE'S RED BICYCLE

The whole quat is talking about it. This story recounts the biography of Pa Moutomè. A true biography. In it, vice and virtue mix. It seems amusing—which it is, to a certain extent. It's one of those pointless stories of no interest that people still tell.

Before the change in his life, Pa Moutomè was a reserved man, a humble peasant who liked hunting, fishing, and the kinds of activities that the people of Bona Mbella recognized as being of worth. That's no longer the case. If you consider Pa Moutomè more closely, you'd swear that he had wished for the misfortune that later swept down on him. Five months ago, his father died. And so his life changed overnight. He found himself at the head of an important inheritance: material goods, wives and their kids, servants, and various other things that had made his father one of the most respected men in the country.

Pa Moutomè also inherited the right to replace his father at meetings of the Wise Men of Bona Mbella. These meetings take place near the beach, under an old baobab whose branches encircle visitors. Pa Moutomè goes there Friday evenings to listen attentively to the council members and observe their reactions. He remains mute throughout the deliberations. At meeting's end, he slips his *sans-confiance* onto his feet—Australian-style flip-flops that give out on you before you reach your destination. He wears his pagne around his waist and pulls an end over his right shoulder, like all the dignitaries do. He takes his leave from the assembly with a deep bow, and he treks home along a grassy path cleared, no doubt, by pigs who sun themselves in the mud of the river that runs behind the houses.

The residence he inherited is an immense building that dominates the huts around it. Shrill echoes escape from it: the voices of women, an integral part of his livestock. The young heir kept his fish business and still devotes himself to hunting and fishing. He's a kind-hearted man; Bona Mbellans praise his generosity. People say his father ripped out his tongue before he died. No one has heard him speak since then.

Late afternoon sunshine, the weather grows mild and fills me with emotion. I observe Pa Moutomè, nonchalance incarnate.

Elegant without making a fuss about it, he walks through the neighborhood like a model, pagne around his waist. Evening is just starting to fall. People are out and about, taking advantage of the breeze. Hand in hand, young girls stroll by. The boys, in groups of four or five, tell each other stories from the day, laughing to the point of embarrassing those around them. But their good humor enlivens the street. Pa Moutomè doesn't attract any attention. He hums the tunes of old-fashioned *yé-yés*. As one of his neighbors says, he thinks he's still in the sixties. His *attitude walk*—an American technique—proves it. He saunters with style. Pa Moutomè is a melancholic. He was born like that, a languid creature. Even Munch's paintings pale in comparison. He trails around, eyes filled with sorrow.

One Saturday, the Caimans—the soccer team from Akwa, a neighboring quat—are going to play against Bona Mbella's only team, the Leopards. Men, women, and children prepare for the match. People are quick with their predictions: "Sparks will fly! We're finally gonna whip 'em!" boom a few voices.

The Bona Mbellans recall the last match between the two teams, an event that caused havoc . . . Pa Moutomè had been among the spectators. He, too, had prepared himself for that unmissable occasion. He'd gotten out his bicycle (he used it only rarely) and painted it bright red so it could be seen from a distance. Pa Moutomè nursed the hope that Bito—a young woman he secretly lusted after—would pass in front of his house. Indeed, to reach the municipal stadium, you had to pass by there . . .

On match days, chaos frightens no one. The quat comes alive, and the atmosphere is charged with the suspense that precedes big fights. People meet up, exchange winks, half-smiles, lovers' rendez-vous. In the courtyards, under the mango trees, they joke about the occasion: "It's gonna be a free-for-all!" say some. "We're gonna give them a thrashing!" rejoice others. The inhabitants of Bona Mbella also recall the events of the last encounter, anecdotes about the Caimans and Leopards. There's an ambiance of laughter that rouses the old people and delights the young girls whose bodies are squeezed into little floral dresses and their feet into gold espadrilles. Their hearts beat to the point of bursting. The match's outcome and romantic passion leave them feeling dazed. Unconsciously, they make coquettish gestures, and thus offer themselves without knowing it to the desire of the young men buzzing around them, hovering like swarms of bees. The dance of seduction occupies an invisible space between the girls and boys: the latter amass tactics to conquer the former. On both sides, they display their merchandise. The lightness in the air promises complete release. Witches ululate in the distance.

The match also creates a panic. Malicious gossip flourishes. The Leopards, who some say are invincible, elicit unkind words. Pa Moutomè, true to form, remains impassive, but his melancholy has become joy. He confronts the week's big adventure, and betrays a certain emotion nonetheless.

Pa Moutomè gets out his bicycle. The man who never says a word to anyone, who is gentle, good, and very practical, escapes the ordinary through his gestures, his bicycle, and the aura of silence that surrounds him. He knows that Bito will pass in in front of his house, accompanied by her best friend. Secretly smitten by Bito's smile, Pa Moutomè goes over in his mind the scenarios that will lead her to share his bed. He has seen her grow up. This Saturday, he spoke to her for the first time, which gave the recipient of his smile the look of someone being brutally torn from her reverie. So he started talking very fast. In the past, he had often left fish on the doorstep of Bito's home. He would accomplish the act without a word and discreetly scan her visitors to locate Bito as she attended to various tasks in the courtyard. It was his way of settling in advance, he thought, the dowry of his future wife.

No one suspected anything: he was always kind and likable, the local bores would have said. A kind mute. But this Saturday was not like the others . . .

Pa Moutomè waits on the front step of his house, certain that Bito and me, her only friend, will pass by there about one o'clock to reach the municipal field. He waits near his bright red bicycle for at least an hour. Not having seen us, he mounts the bicycle and heads to the stadium.

He suddenly spies us and almost falls flat on his face. He immediately suggests to Bito that he take her to the municipal field. At heart, the big mute is nothing but a big weakling. And so he trembles with fear and shame. A little smile creases the corners of his mouth.

"You don't even say hello to us, you just ask me if I want to get on your bike? Just like that?"

"Oh, sorry, girls! Good evening, are you going to the field?"

"Yes."

"Me too. And I bet, Bito, that you've never been on a bicycle . . ."

"No, actually."

"Well then, get on. I'll take you there!"

Excited to no end, a naïve Bito gets on the bicycle without asking my opinion, ditching me on the spot. I have trouble digesting the scene: already a few suspicions insinuate themselves into my mind.

Pa Moutomè and Bito ride away rather quickly. He whistles, she smiles in wonder. After a few streets, Pa Moutomè drops by his house again, still with Bito, under that pretext that he needs some money to buy beer after the match. Bito follows him, uncomfortable, but not wanting to annoy the person who has given her a wondrous fifteen minutes.

Hardly has Bito set foot inside the house than Pa Moutomè throws himself at the door and locks it shut. Having closed her in, he goes to see the match alone, satisfied with himself.

With no remorse, he watches the match, even though he's ravaged by passion. And I leave the match alone. The Caimans lost, and Bona Mbella is celebrating. I miss the friend I normally comment on the match with, and I complain about it. I go straight to Bito's house, since night has fallen. Her mother, surprised to see me without her daughter, asks in bewilderment, "Well, where's Bito?"

I hesitate for a moment and then say that Pa Moutomè picked her up on his bicycle.

"What? You must be joking. No, that's impossible!"

It's late and Bito's father still hasn't returned. He's in his favorite bar drinking with his friends. After matches, there's an open door policy on the greatest excess. They drink to the point of rolling into waterholes.

Bito's mother leaves her house, accompanied by her brother and her youngest son. The four of us arrive at Pa Moutomè's, but he refuses to open up.

"Where's my niece? You don't know anything about all this?" Bito's uncle exclaims. "Really now, no one steals women these days! You can't be serious!"

Insults are exchanged and all manner of threats, but Pa Moutomè is determined not to open the door. Throughout, Bito pulls a long face; she has the look of a young girl kidnapped by her future husband.

The next day, Bito's father, followed by several neighbors, sets off for Pa Moutomè's to get his daughter back. Following lengthy negotiations, Bito's father and the others decide to go to court to make a complaint of child abduction: Bito's only seventeen.

"Why not have a trial right here!" says one of the uncles. "Court proceedings are long and complicated. Personally, I think he's guilty."

The Wise Men's council assembles: Pa Moutomè is guilty. He's invited to explain himself.

"But Pa Moutomè can't speak," someone observes.

"Since Bito's abduction, he's regained his speech," replies one of the wise men. "Unbelievable but true, the mute speaks! Long live the ancestors!"

The oldest wise man intervenes: "Pa Moutomè has found himself a wife. Is that the issue?"

"Of course not. He also has to pay the dowry and apologize to the family," another suggests. "After all, as far as the young woman goes, you could classify him as a pedophile, but between us, this practice is well known among the ancestors. You carry off the woman who's softened your heart, and that's that!"

Another uncle demands he pay an elevated dowry. Pa Moutomè is no fool. He understands that the family is asking him for money.

He mutters proudly into his beard, "Just like in *The Iliad*, I'm a woman-thief, like Paris who carried off Helen from Agamemnon. Yes, me!"

"What an adventure! What wizardry!" concludes Chantou with a burst of laughter.

Pa Moutomè has a clear conscience. The very night of the abduction, Bito became his wife. Noblesse oblige, he apologized for the disorder he had caused and committed to paying the dowry requested for the rites of marriage.

Bito's family sulk, but they have no choice. Bito gives them their first grandson nine months later. She became Pa

Moutomè's wife almost without noticing it. Eleven children were born from the marriage, all of them handsome and full of life. At school, the other children insult them by calling their father a thief.

"Ravishing women is an archaic phenomenon," recalls the old woman who serves as the quat's doyenne.

Everybody agrees in silence. They say an old person is a library. And this story rests in archives that hold the history of the children of Bona Mbella.

PANÈ

I

Panè is a star, and the light that we share over the course of the night is like a gift from the heavens. Everybody in Bona Mbella is talking about her. The mystery around her person inclines us to make the most varied allusions, to spiritualism for example, or mysticism, or even to the isthmus of her impregnable secret. She is the astounding image of a no less astounding planet: Bona Mbella, our neighborhood, or, as its inhabitants call it, the quat. She comes from elsewhere. Today, her contribution to our lives is among the most appreciated. Panè is in the business of *makala ma mbasi*, cornflour fritters. She sells them like the host to the blessed. And she sings . . .

What bliss to eat fresh makala ma mbasi! Or rather, warm ones. We always treat ourselves to them, my sisters and I. Panè kneads the dough with loving care. Although she smiles readily, she never breathes a word, except when she's humming—which is nearly all the time—from either joy or pain. Words and sounds fill her throat, aerating it.

Panè sings when she doesn't have any customers, a melody that attracts passersby who then become her clients. The song arises from a lack of consumers but just as quickly creates them. They stop just to listen, and soon there's a crowd around the golden makala ma mbasi, the joy of the early morning workers. When Panè lifts her head from her frying, she sees all the eyes around her little oven, devouring her.

Every morning the same monotonous tune regulates her gestures. Panè lights the fire and begins to cook the makala ma mbasi at six o'clock, and soon people are thronging around her. At that early hour, Panè is already wearing brightly colored lipstick. She's always decked out like an actress about to be whisked straight on stage for scenes she has no need to rehearse.

I observe her from a distance. She poses voluptuously. I wonder whether she sleeps in a low-cut red dress, just like the one now revealing the tattoo on her left shoulder. I love that dress: it shows off her heavy breasts and slims her waist.

When I buy makala ma mbasi from Panè, I stare at her like forbidden fruit. I try to catch the eye of that most beautiful of strangers. Sometimes I gaze at her for hours on end before I finally go up to give my order: five corn makala ma mbasi, and not one less! My daily ration. Her mouth draws me in like some kind of obscene suction cup. I tremble when her eyes rest on me. Everything about her captivates me. Excited by her tattoo, I'd like to run my finger over the contours of her skin, slide slowly over its surface, the magic stuff of dreams. A little red bird with an indigo beak is etched on her shoulder. I call it the *fledgling of love*. It's a mark addressed to her admirers. I understand her love for low-cut dresses: they serve her intentions so well. One morning, while the usual crowd surrounded her, I took advantage of a narrow passage to place myself directly in front of her, then circled behind. Instead of looking at her mouth, I slipped to the back of the stall for a better view of her tattoo. Her shoulder moved to the rhythm of her voice. That's how I auscultated her tattoo . . .

With a body as impassioned as hers, so to speak, I imagine that she never removes her red beret. It actually hides the contours of her newly shaven head, and I have only one desire: to see her head without its covering. Women who adopt this hairstyle are rare, aside from the Bamilékés who do so to honor their dead. Panè appropriated a sign of mourning and then she embellished it, which makes her gesture all the more sensual. I'd like to leave the fragrance of my lips upon it.

Once I arranged to be alone with her. It was the end of the morning, and she was tidying up her things, humming those melancholy tunes that remind me of sad childhood mornings. In a steady voice I tell her—her surprise is obvious—that my name is Chantou, that I find her appealing and would like to be her friend. She gradually lifts her head and stares at me. She looks me right in the eyes, a twinkle in the corner of hers. With pursed lips, she nods her head. I can't bear her looking at me. I'm ashamed and beat a quick retreat. I just stand there while she finishes putting away her things. She collects her basin, places it on her head, and launches into a new melody with a gait that makes her whole body dance. I follow her, exalted, terrified, but conquered.

I've often studied women's backsides in the street. It reminds me of *Quartier Mozart*, the film by Jean-Pierre Bekolo. The actress—Saturday is her name—is going to join her mother who sells rice and beans. That's how she provides for the workers' noontime break. Battered and turned out from her conjugal home, the mother has to support herself. Her daughter Saturday, who often thinks about her mother, tries to get back in contact with her. One day, she decides to help her. When the mother finishes clearing up her business, Saturday places a basin on her head, and adopts the nonchalant rhythm of her mother's steps.

When Panè isn't selling makala ma mbasi, she's out walking, wiggling her hips. Her backside is beyond compare! In the afternoons, she sings in a choir. As in all the Bona Mbella choirs, there's a required dress, in addition to the one for special occasions: funerals, baptisms, and tontines, where women meet to make their savings bear fruit. Panè's the only member of the choir who doesn't wear a uniform. Because she refused the compulsory dress, they decreed her to be the exception. The truth is that they can't manage without her voice. She shows up in sometimes ill-fitting outfits of a strange red hue. Everyone inspects her in silence, not knowing what to say to her—they look down on her even as they admire her.

When she open her mouth, she touches hearts, floods faces with joy. At the end of her performance, comments come thick and fast, though no one dares speak to her in person. She never responds anyway. Her voice is a daily litany, a lament for wounded hearts. Nothing seems to reach her. On the contrary, you feel a certain uneasiness in trying to get involved with her. She surrenders herself only in song.

Watching her walk in her red high heels is a treat. They make her calves look sublime. The rounded form of the latter make the former look all the more shiny. Panè's in love with her skin, which she cares for like a golden goose. She's proud of it—why wouldn't she be? Just from the way she walks, you can feel her joie de vivre. Her aura makes me tremble like a leaf in the wind.

The same scene repeats itself every morning. Standing before the obscure object of my desires, I quiver and lose my voice. Slowly, I advance: even from a distance it's important that I sense her body beneath the oily spray of her frying. Actually, it's only in dreams that I act or think I act that way. Blinking my eyes, I come out of my torpor. I belong to the invisible and visible world at the same time. Even my guardian angel knows it. I'm imperceptible. Only the memory of what I am helps me escape ambivalence, momentarily.

There are people who touch you right in your heart. A strange harmony emanates from them. Their extravagance is imposing. Panè is one of them. She was fashioned from a matchless mold.

Panè never asks anyone for anything. She lives in a little house made from *carabote*, scrap lumber, also painted red. The curtains, which you can see from behind the grilled windows, are of the same color. Set right in the middle of houses that are painted white, her little place catches your eye. There's no courtyard, just a little space between her house and the neighbors. Panè, disengaged as she is from any social idiocies, lives her life as she sees fit. She's the bird on its branch—a singular branch, of course. She pays for it with unparalleled solitude. *Lady Bird*, that's what she is. Free of tensions, rumors, and gossip, her heart beats to its own rhythm. I want to love her just as she appears.

Tongues certainly wag about her silence. Not only is this strange beauty the object of her own passion, but also of the entire neighborhood, and of me in particular. She takes no notice, does as she pleases, remains completely impervious to other people's nasty curiosity. Her dream? To live far from the cries of misery and hate that obsess her. Her past? Who knows!

Here's what happened one afternoon. An old woman suddenly appeared, and the population reached the height of agitation because no one knew her identity. She was dressed in red from head to toe, exactly like Panè. This detail would surely shed some light on Panè, the scarlet-colored beauty. The old woman dragged her withered body to the working-class bar and settled in. She asked for a beer from everyone who came inside. It was the only way she knew to cool off. Her appearance inspired some degree of fear, but no one dared tell her to leave since she bore such a close resemblance to the *Juju du Rond Pont Bona Mbella*, a statue—which nobody much cared for—planted in the town center. The barman, tired of seeing her approach people who only ignored her, finally offered her a cold beer: she drank it in one go. The bottle empty, she asked her benefactor, "Do you know Panè?"

He nodded his head yes. "Panè sells delicious makala in the neighborhood. Plus she's got a wonderful voice. If you want to meet her, just show up at her stall. She's there every morning." The little old woman asked if she could have another beer, on credit this time. The barman let out a hearty laugh. "My dear lady, we don't give credit here anymore! Mr. Free Credit is dead. It's been five years at least! And where've you come from anyway? You're embarrassing me with your rags, and on top of that you smell bad. Don't you have any children to take care of you? I'll ask one of my little ones to take you to our place. My wife will look after you. Go on, she'll wash you and give you a nice, clean *kaba* dress."

The old woman was delighted: for once someone was pampering her. But while the server felt sorry for her, the clients looked disconcerted as they came and went. They peered at her like a bunch of beggars.

People ignored Panè because she frightened them. Even her neighbors didn't keep company with her. But the old woman had sparked a contagious curiosity. People scrutinized her. The attention made her nostalgic, and she struck up a sad aria. Reserved at first, the old woman's voice intensified until it drew a crowd. Everyone took it for Panè, but since she never set foot in the bars, astonishment gave way to stupefaction. Where was the voice coming from? From which woman's body? From which organ? These questions led to still more questions, which only amplified the general uneasiness. The old woman sang to the point of exhaustion. The barman was staggered by the state of the cash register. The more enthusiastic the customers became, the more they drank.

The manager offered a beer to the little old woman, who was again delighted. Someone brought her a meal that she gulped down with gusto. The boss had one of his sons called and asked him to bring her to their home. The old woman agreed to wash herself but refused the kaba. Testily, she demanded a red one.

"Really now, why red?" exclaimed her hosts.

"Because it's me! It's the color of the blood of my ancestors." Her plea impressed them. They found her a piece of red pagne cloth with a blouse of the same color. They also left a piece of a mat at her disposal, but they made sure it matched her clothing. Pleased with her treatment, she started to sing again. The children fell asleep instantly, lulled by her song. The voice of the unknown woman was the kind that fills you with contentment. She was an ephemeral being; her body, which seemed lighter to us than a sparrow feather, didn't actually exist at all. She leapt from rooftop to rooftop, like a bat. She clung to the eaves to watch over the quat.

From up there, her eyes dazzled the children. She was our guardian angel. There are days when tragedy surprises us, we others, we mortals. Cries from the slums slice through the neighborhood. She, our fairy, is the only one who listens to all these cries while she sings. By her melodies, she protects us; by her watching, she wards off evils spells. "Fight to survive," she calls out from the heights of her vigil.

It was a tranquil night. The barman and his family awoke refreshed, but a big surprise awaited them: the little old woman had disappeared. Just where could she be? They searched everywhere. Bona Mbella was in an uproar. The news spread like a powder trail. People wanted to find her and listen to her sing one more time. So the neighborhood turned to Panè. The little old woman had uttered her name several times. And a couple of other things connected the two women: the color red and that bit of angelic voice. People gave in to all manner of speculation. But the commotion reached its peak when they realized that Panè herself had also disappeared. She had sold her makala ma mbasi that very morning, but normally she sang in the choir in the afternoon, and she hadn't turned up. While people discussed all of these coincidences, I was given information by a mysterious voice. Someone or something confided in my ear, "Panè and the little old woman are *édimos*." Édimos? "But those are invisible beings! How could Panè have lived among us for so many years if she were an édimo? You'd think we would have noticed!"

To be sure, the quat and the world had really changed. In Bona Mbella, when I was a child, there hadn't been such confusion. An édimo? Anyway, the word was taboo. Édimos signify invisibility, the silence at work in the spirit world. As soon as their presence is felt—or noticed by some sign—they disappear for a good long while, only to reappear later in a form stripped of all its appeal.

Well, let's say that I was doomed to speculate. First I have to establish what édimos really look like. Who hasn't seen a film where some édimos traumatize a whole crowd of people? Films like that bring unusual phenomena into play. At the end of the day, it's not really as convincing as all that. We'd only have learned that we like stories that remind us of the thrill of our childhood fears. Let's allow silence to flow back into us, then.

Contrary to all expectation, the next morning Panè was there, sitting on her little bench as usual. People first came toward her simply out of routine, but then they sincerely wanted to see and talk to her. Rumor had spread the news about her true condition. But very few people bought any makala ma mbasi that day. They were afraid and kept silent. Panè continued to poke her fire, and then she started to sing. In any case, her makala ma mbasi would sell themselves. People came a long way just to buy them. Recent events had made her voice more beautiful than ever. Her cantilena filled people's hearts with sumptuous feelings. Imagine Nina Simone belting out "Feeling Good." As a matter of fact, the American woman sings sadness to calm our anxieties. Nina Simone, like Panè, sings cries for help.

Today, Panè's charms are barely working. Even the morning customers are hesitant to approach. In order to hand them their purchase and collect the money, Panè has to lean over. The clients keep their distance. Her spell is fading, but she can still count on the spell of her delicious fritters. Panè, not deviating from her usual composure, endeavors to remain serene. The aloofness of her usual customers benefits those who usually arrive too late to get any. But neither hangs around after they've paid. For the other vendors, it's their lucky day. They don't go home empty-handed.

Between two songs, a vague, nearly contemptuous smile plays across Panè's lips. She won't let herself be beaten down by their pettiness. But I know it hurts her, and her pain registers in her voice. My stomach is in knots. So many torments, and no one to guess at them. I feel a womanly love for her.

Sita Ndomè's arrival in the quat revived in Panè the whole of her buried life story, and little by little, memories resurfaced. How, then, to reconstruct all the scattered pieces of her past?

Panè tells her story.

II

The shadow of a secret hovers over the village of Mpongo. People no doubt remember the day when the blood of my assailants finally flowed. The three murderers were tossed into the same hole, a pile of spare body parts, chunks of naked flesh. Such was the fate of those who assaulted my childhood. They were each short a member.

The villagers awoke to this horrific spectacle. They repressed everything until they became as silent as the grave. No one understood how I could massacre three men who had sound bodies though small minds. I severed their members and displayed them on the square. That was the day of my rebirth. There was nothing else I could have done. I didn't have a choice. The only way to take on terror is to abandon yourself to it.

So let the police guard those scraps of flesh, and let the villagers ponder their own abjection. They witnessed my ordeal, and they didn't lift a finger. What can you expect from people like that? Nothing. Anyway, no one cried. They were just astonished by the dishonor that had befallen them. "What will the neighboring villages say?" was their only reaction. But then they changed their minds: the others were just as cowardly as they were. Everyone knew what children, young girls, women had to endure. They kept silent, even though they were bursting with remorse. They told themselves, "Let the secret be kept as long as the ancestors shall live." But every secret, whatever it may be, is uncovered someday.

The past lives in us, even if I claim to be healed of it. I swam in my blood the day I was raped. My blood is a river. I swim, with finstrokes, in its red waters.

On the black slate of my memory, the sharp outline of a friendly face appears.

Listen, Chantou, I fascinate you, but it's not worth the trouble. Find another friend. I've got nothing to offer you. I ended up in Bona Mbella trying to flee a dreadful history. I hit bottom—I don't think there's a worse experience than the one I lived through. That's why when I sing my pain, I'm also singing my hatred. I never smiled a child's luminous smile. From the beginning, mine conveyed disaster. In the village, Sita Ndomè—I'll tell you about her later—was my only recourse.

Chantou, it wasn't all just a bad dream. The evidence is this: the suffering never leaves me now. It reverberates in my voice, as if to remind me of the initial wound. Eventually I tattooed my survival: the red bird bending over my shoulder. I'm the paddling fish and the bird taking flight. My pain has been avenged, so I can fake forgetfulness.

Chantou, I was told an old woman in red rags asked after me. I'll tell you about her, though my life isn't for telling. It carries me sometimes toward even crueler horizons. I've always left the talking to others. Those busybodies don't know that my life's just one big mess . . .

Sita Ndomè came to visit me. She wanted to judge for herself the treatment the neighborhood people reserve for me. Sita Ndomè blessed me at my birth. She held me in her arms and whispered these words into my ear: "You'll be the star that will reawaken the dead and replenish hearts with joy. You'll be a helpmate for the women who mend socks. You'll be the voice that revives hope and the hand that applies balm to wounds. You'll predict the future of a whole generation of children born in war."

Yesterday, some jerk called out aggressively, "Hey, don't you know that a little old lady who sings exactly like you turned up here and the next day flew off without leaving a trace?" At first I wanted to wall myself up in silence. Then I sang so that beauty would take hold of the shouter's heart. "Give me 200 francs worth of makala ma mbasi, you," he said. "You're strange. You never talk to your customers. What's your problem? We'll know the truth one day. Your makala are too good—there's something suspicious in all of this."

Panè's tale left me pensive, and I gaze at her devotedly. She hands her customers a plate and collects the money without saying a word. That morning, people ask her a thousand questions: "Do you know the mysterious lady from yesterday?" Panè doesn't answer; instead she sings to herself *mezzo voce*—an eternity of blues . . .

Then Panè resumed the thread of her story.

When I was in Mpongo, I lived in fear. I replied to people cavalierly, since I mistrusted the questions they asked me. There are some things you share and others you keep quiet about. If silence terrifies some people, malicious gossip hurts others. And me, Panè, I tell them to take silence's side. Look, it's like that girl who's always after me, Chantou. She gazes at me adoringly. She wants to understand me. If I told her my story, wouldn't she run away? How can I tell her that terror has condemned me to silence? She's only a child after all.

Today, I'm twenty-eight years old. My legs have stopped shaking. And the tortures of the soul are over and done with. I try my hardest to forget, I relax. My life is less intense, but also more pleasant. People appreciate me, if only for my song. No one looked at me before. I used to cry every night in Sita Ndomè's hut. I committed murder at the age of eleven, and my rape goes back to when I was seven. Since then, shadows have become my home.

Sita Ndomè gave me her breast until I was five, when she went to sleep forever. She used to sing songs to me every day. She introduced me to vocal exercises. Sita Ndomè was a good, smiling woman with an impeccable appearance. She sewed my dresses herself. Each one had matching ribbons for my hair. "You're my child," she used to tell me. She didn't have any of her own. My mother gave birth into her arms before breathing her last. Misfortune welcomed me into its cradle. When my second mother disappeared as well, I found myself at the neighbors', just because of proximity. I never met a single member of my family. Neither before or since.

III

Sita Ndomè visits me regularly in my dreams, especially when I'm in despair, like on the day I was first raped. It was morning, and the weather was cool. Sita Ndomè suddenly appeared and began to sing to me. She told me to take my suffering patiently. "One day you'll be freed," she murmured. But that day didn't come. I was raped by all the men of the house: Mota Loko, his son, and Sango Kouta.

It's the rainy season, and it's coming down in buckets. People are shut up in their houses. Like every day, I'm coming back from the market, but earlier than usual. It's the rule: parents advise their children to return as soon as possible to avoid the raging currents of water. At the Lokos' house, I have to sell *miondos*, manioc sticks, to eat my fill. I learned to make them when I was seven. The Lokos own vast fields of manioc where I work for my daily ration. My job is to go to the field, pull up some manioc, soak it in large basins, clean it, and then knead the dough for the miondos. I don't like going to the fields alone—I'm afraid of meeting spirits. But Sita Ndomè whispers in my ear: *Don't worry, I'll help you! We'll work together! It's nothing!*

On that fateful day, I've just set down my three packets of twenty miondos each when someone strikes me on the shoulder so hard that I wind up flat on my back. I hadn't seen anyone coming—the house was in shadow. There I am spread out, him on top of me, and his member erect, tearing me apart. Sobs choke my throat. I'm in pain, and I scream as loud as I can, but no one's there to save me. There's blood everywhere, on the ground, my dress. When he's finished, he tells me to go get some of the local gin, *haa*, for him at *Bon pour tous*, Credit for All. It's hard for me to walk, and he kicks me so that I tumble to the ground in the muddy courtyard. Lying on the ground, I hear Sita's voice: "Go get the haa. And above all, don't say a word to anyone. Get up, don't cry. There're lots of people under the tent at *Bon pour tous*. They'll take care of you."

I show up at the little bistro which is run by a woman I don't know, not even her name. Maybe she's called *Bon pour tous* like her bistro?

When she sees me, she literally falls to pieces. She takes me by the hand and leads me to her room where she removes my dress, dries me off, and consoles me. "Don't cry, my girl. It's over." She's furious, and her eyes are on fire. She swears, speaking rapidly in a language I don't understand. My disaster has sparked her anger. I still can't manage to say anything. I'm suffocating.

Helplessness takes hold of us both. We remain speechless for a good long while, a pose that today reminds me of the reproduction of a painting that a customer forgot at my stall one morning. I kept it hoping the client would return. After a few weeks, he showed up and acknowledged that it was a gift for me. He wanted the somber colors of the painting to contrast with my eternal blood-red. It's *The Scream*, 1893, a painting by Edvard Munch. A scream that tears my vocal chords . . .

Verbal unrest is part of the world where I grew up. Laughter and violence, life and death. In my mind's eye, I see the movements of that woman searching for a dress among her clothing. I hear her suppressed revolt. Her words sound in my ear like the screeching of an old train's axles. Images of horror follow one after the other in my head. The woman fills a bottle with stinking liquid and spits into it several times as she curses the Lokos. I go back out into the rain with her. In spite of my discomfort, I try to keep up with her quick pace. Her strides betray her fury. Once we arrive at the Lokos', my benefactress goes into the shack, which is still plunged in shadow.

"Mota Loko, come out of your room. I know you're in there. Come out! I saw what you did to this little girl. I'll tell your wife. Aren't you ashamed, an old man like you?"

The owner of *Bon pour tous* screams like a militant. She slams the door as she leaves, shouting, "What a bunch of imbeciles!" I wait outside for Mota Loko's wife to return. I know very well that he'll beat both of us like he usually does, but I'm still going to tell her what happened. Mota Loko's wife never talks about her miseries, but she sheds streams of tears. Her son also beats her, just like his father, and insults her in public from time to time. For the son, his mother is nothing but a whore, a slut who dirties his father's name. One day I saw him climb on top of his mother. He screws her just like his father does.

Before, I didn't really understand the realities of the family. I don't reflect on it anymore. In the village, people whispered that the Lokos were cursed, but they were the only ones who took me in of their own accord after Sita Ndomè's death. The fact that our houses were connected had something to do with it maybe. I still don't understand the meaning of their hospitality. And yet people say that a child can't be abandoned in our villages . . . The woman from *Bon pour tous* lavished a few consoling caresses on me, and Sita loved me, loves me still.

I often go to hide in my second mother's hut. I stay there for hours. It's the only place where I can escape my godfamily. One day another neighbor, Sango Kouta, bursts in on me there. He says, "I know you give yourself to Mota Loko. Well, everybody knows. If you don't let me have my piece, too, I'll tell all the men in the neighborhood to jump you." I look at him, terrified. He turns me over on the mat and mounts on top of me. He shudders a moment and then I hear a big grunt. It doesn't hurt. It's not like the other time. The pain of my first rape was indescribable. Since then, Mota Loko has taken me regularly when he returned from the field or the market. While Sango Kouta rapes me, the voice of Sita Ndomè rocks me with its melodies.

I've finally had enough: "Do something, Sita Ndomè, I can't take it anymore! Do something!" While I despair about my fate, I see—as if in a dream—my wet nurse hanging from the ceiling. Sango Kouta, who also took to fucking me regularly, is crushing me with his weight. I yell with all my might. Sita Ndomè, finger to her lips, urges me to keep quiet. She continues to hang from the ceiling like a bat, and she sings to me until Sango Kouta has finally ejaculated. Satisfied with the job he's done, he grabs his pagne cloth and leaves. Sita Ndomè, still fixed to the archway, swears that these men will pay one day for what they've done to me. "That will be a great day for all the young girls of the world," she tells me. Sita Ndomè is preparing a blow for them that will really shock their sensibilities.

I tell her in a strangled voice, "Hurry, Sita Ndomè, I can't take it anymore! You know, there're three of them who mount on top of me now. The younger Loko, called Muna Loko, is the latest recruit. Tell me, do the ancestors listen to me? During the wake for Madame *Bon pour tous*, Muna Loko seized me by the arm and dragged me out to rape me behind the bistro. I screamed well enough, but no one moved. There was a real commotion that night . . . Sita Ndomè, I want to be with you again. I hate them all. They're going to drive me mad with their penises as black as charcoal. Get me out of this hell. I can't take it anymore. I've suffered too much already. Take me . . . Even the lady from *Bon pour tous* has left this world. The day of her burial, I cried and cried. Every now and then, she used to caress my ears with sweet words. She was full of kindness."

At the wake, a few people with eyes bloodshot from lack of sleep quit listening to the griotte. She stopped abruptly, took a deep breath, and resumed her song. I listen as though dazzled . . . The griotte seems sincere. Each word that falls from her lips penetrates to the core of me. Her stories fill me with joy. I'm reborn. Her art fascinates me. I listen, I watch her, she smiles . . .

Mota Loko's wife disappeared as well. She committed suicide and was found hanging from a tree as if she'd been lynched. A suicide in the village was unimaginable. We were at the edge of the abyss for sure. Madame Loko is no longer to be pitied—she finally triumphed over her humiliation. Like smoke, little by little, her shadow dissipates. But I'm still stuck with these brutes. Tomorrow they'll finish me off as well with their oversized penises that reach almost up to my throat. That Sango Kouta, for example. Not only has he got a long thing, but his stomach is as fat as a woman's who's about to give birth.

But there's Sita. I hear her voice. She's preparing to intervene. Patience, she murmurs, is the key to my deliverance. Days pass without any precise message. I don't know what I'm supposed to do. I'd like to contemplate the stars like all the other children in the world. I imagine my family as an ocean. I plunge in to drown myself there . . .

I'm in agony.

Have they changed their mores? In everyone's eyes I've become the official mistress of the Loko house. I cook, wash their clothing, take care of all the tasks usually allotted to housewives, including going to the beds of these messieurs—father and son, friends and cronies—to satisfy their desires. I'm a child of eleven, and my body has been raped for four years. I've had enough. Their sperm is rotting my insides. They stink and they're filling me with it. I want to fly off like a bird. Far away from them, I'll invent a happy past, a mixture of ocean, birds, and multicolored fish.

I grew up a live wire, but I've become as hard as stone. Nothing unsettles me anymore. My heart is black with hate; it dried up my tears. Over the years, my body has started hurting less. Even with Kouta: he only makes my uterus suffer for a moment since he ejaculates quickly. His pelvic thrusts are a real ordeal. He penetrates me in a few quick prods and then backs out with a grunt worse than the death rattle of an animal having its throat cut. No matter if I wash myself in lemon, the smell of his sperm, sweat, and alcohol still cling to my skin. My despair grows in measure.

The daily routine of the village reminds me of the life I used to lead with Sita Ndomè. I think of the childhood that slipped away from me like an illusion. When I pass by, an unusual silence seizes the villagers who gaze at me dumbly.

Nothing is said on the subject of me. Apparently, though I live among them, I am, in fact, invisible. Now I have all the attributes of a young woman. The little girl who stayed in her corner, puny and withdrawn, reveals her merits: little breasts as round as lemons, noble breasts. I'm a woman for real.

That afternoon, I arrive as usual at the choir where no one has spoken to me since. They know not to bother me. If they want me to cooperate, it's in their best interest to leave me alone. So I sing.

I've arrived early. I'm waiting for the program for the day's rehearsal. I stare at the ceiling like in the shacks where they rape me. I think of those times when I've seen Sita Ndomè. She looks at me the same way as before. I notice that she has new clothes. I smile. She presses her finger to her lips to bid me to be silent. I want to talk to her, ask her advice. She keeps me company until the beginning of the first song. Her presence alters my mood. I feel better, less alone. It softens the fact that the whole neighborhood has taken a sudden disliking to me. People look at me with hostility, and some isolate me completely.

From time to time, I converse with Sita Ndomè. I explain to her how I pull my weight in the choir since I sing with all my heart! As I return home, I keep singing. I take my time, walk slowly: I'm happy.

The wind blows on my face. I feel men looking at me, which gives me even more of an urge to wiggle my hips. As long as I only worry about myself, I'm peaceful. All that whispering doesn't get to me. You shouldn't have anything to do with people devoid of sympathy.

For me, this gray morning is an exceptional one. I feel my life turning upside down. Even though I'm more alone than ever, I know I can count on Sita Ndomè. My makala ma mbasi have been prepared with loving care. Sita Ndomè watches me mix the corn batter with bananas and salt. I learned all that from her. She gave me everything: courage, energy, hope, life. When I think of her, my heart swells with gratitude. I feel soothed, overcome with kindness.

IV

On this dull, rainy day, a surprise is waiting for me, the girl who ever since has felt shielded from misfortune. I hear voices again, one of which is Sita's. They all pronounce the same words, state the same request. Has the moment finally arrived for me to face my destiny? Sita, true to herself, tells me to wait and bear it.

Outside, the bad weather degenerates into a fierce rain. Everyone runs for cover. People returning from their errands are soaked to the bone. I go into Sita's hut, where I light a fire. As head of the premises, Sango Kouta bursts in without warning. He is reinvesting in a property that speaks to him in a familiar language. I huddle in front of the hearth. He says something to me. I'm hardly breathing, my chest tight. Since I don't respond, he moves closer. His wet clothes cling to his enormous bulk. He knocks into me, but his fat stomach and poorly fitting pagne cloth hinder his movement. Nimbly I retreat from the fireside. It's the first time I've given any indication of resisting. I look up at the ceiling, hoping to catch sight of Sita. She isn't there. A knot forms in my throat. My legs are giving out, with the weight of the world bearing down on my shoulders.

Sango Kouta gives a long, nervous laugh. Panic-stricken, my eyes scan the room in every direction. Still no sign from the ceiling. "I'm looking for you, Sita, come quick!" Sango Kouta is talking in a surly voice, but the words get caught in his throat so that he's practically stammering. I'm not listening to him. I know now that he'll never touch me again—I've just decided. To urge myself to stay calm, I recite prayers to myself. The smoke is fading, the fire gradually dying. Half-glowing embers flare up from time to time. I feed them by adding bits of wood. It's in gathering the wood that I spy an arrow on the door. Puzzled, I go over to examine it more closely and immediately stop praying. For a brief instant, I forget my nightmare. I rekindle the fire and plant myself in front of it. Sango Kouta comes at me, bellowing. I turn my head away. Every fiber of my body is tensed. He leaps on me like a wildcat. It feels like an electric shock when his skin touches mine. Three hundred volts shake my body. I don't know how or when an enormous bat swept into the shack. Kouta-le-Grand spots the beast which, miraculously, looks him straight in the eye. Sango Kouta sputters some swear words that make me smile. I take advantage of the moment to snatch the arrow and conceal it nearby. Then I lie down on the mat, my legs spread apart, ready to receive him.

Sango Kouta notices what position I'm in. A big grin distorts his face. My heart is in knots, and I'm overcome with hatred.

"Ah, I knew you were just pretending to resist me! No woman can resist a man, especially not a little girl like you. One more reason for you to give in to me without negotiation. Now that you've got cute little breasts, you want to act like the big girls. You'll see what Sango Kouta is going to do to you. With this cursed rain, I need to warm myself up."

"Well, hurry up then! I'm waiting!"

"Since when do you talk to me like that? Have we raised pigs together? Come on now . . ."

Lying on my back, I finally glimpse Sita Ndomè hanging from the ceiling, a finger raised to her lips. Sita takes out a sharp, shining object from her pagne. She performs a series of gestures, showing me how to proceed. I understand that it's a matter of driving the arrow into the buttock in one swift blow. Sango doesn't even have time to sprawl on top of me. I strike him with the first blow that should, I hope, finish him once and for all. He falls to the side of me, a cry of pain assailing the air instead of his usual grunt. Blood spurts. I stand up, firmly tug the arrow from where it's stuck into his stomach, and jab it into his left buttock. The blow falters against some plump flesh, and the arrow bends slightly. Sango Kouta screams again and again. He tries to speak, but his pain prevents him. He's stammering as usual, and his words are broken. And with all this rain, no one will hear us—the resounding music of the rain is on my side. I continue my carnage with a furor that surprises me. I thrust the arrow wherever I can, and then I pull it out and thrust it in again. Blood spurts with each round trip. Sango Kouta isn't yelling anymore. Maybe he's dead or passed out. Too bad for him. I leave the shack covered in blood. I stand under the rain. I'm shivering all over.

I advance with heavy steps as if to signal the danger my arrival represents for the Loko household. The father is home and hears me enter. He tells me to come into his room, where he's stretched out on a mat. Aggressively, he orders me to go fetch him something to drink from *Bon pour tous*. I take the bottle and recede into the pounding rain. Since the owner's death, another woman—surely some relative— is in charge of the business. I ask her to fill the bottle with haa and put in on the Lokos' account. She doesn't even look at me.

"Little one, we don't give credit anymore. You've got to pay cash! Money, *kayas, dos*! There are new rules."

The woman does her best to explain the new management philosophy to me. She sends me away, asking me to explain it all to my father.

"I don't have a father, or a mother, brother, or sister. I'm alone in the world. My mother died giving birth."

"That's got nothing to do with me, little one. Off you go! Don't forget to pass the message on to that old grump who sent you. Be careful of the rain, don't fall. The currents are swift, and there are huge pools of water. Actually, you should wait here a little while. It's dangerous."

I set off again under the downpour, making a detour to Sita's hut where I glance at my victim. Sango Kouta is bathing in his blood. I grab the arrow and leave again, relieved.

The elder Loko is surely getting impatient. Brusquely, I shove open the door and spout off what the new manager had to say.

"Go look for Petit. At least my son'll know how to buy me something to drink."

I point out what the weather is like, and he gets annoyed.

"Since when do you talk back like that when I'm speaking to you?"

But I insist: "It's a deluge out there. I'm going to wait until the storm passes."

"You're laying it on thick, you little cow! Come here right now! Lie down there. I see your breasts are itching. Since when do you refuse to do my errands? Are your little tits going to your head? Do you think you're a woman or something? Come on, quick, lie down. I'll show you what we do to women, real women with real breasts."

I'm dripping with water. I lie down, and then him on top of me, but my soaking wet body aggravates him. With a slap, he signals me to go dry off. I comply, using the opportunity to retrieve the arrow. Sita isn't far, and again she shows me which movements to make. The elder Loko turns toward me and undoes his pagne. At the moment he's going to penetrate me, I thrust the arrow into his buttock. He screams, swears in Duala, "*À té mba é! À loba lam!*" which means "Poor me! My God!"

"Yes, well you should have thought of that earlier. The ancestors can't do anything for you. You're going to feel the same pain you've inflicted on me for years!"

Outside, the rain is coming down in sheets, and we're terribly alone. The elder Loko cries for help. "No one will come, you sad creature!" I tell him. I carry on piercing him through like a lunatic. Each blow makes me feel good. An incredible feeling of sang-froid overtakes me, sustains the beating of my heart, guides my hand. Loko yells for a long time in a pool of scarlet, and then it's quiet. I take a deep breath. Sita isn't there anymore, and I need some comfort. I pick up the arrow again and leave. The rain cleanses me. I walk for a while, my mind wandering. I already feel better for having spilled that blood.

The rain doesn't stop—on the contrary it reverberates so loudly that it sounds like it's boring through the heavy aluminum roofs. The roar of the water frightens the villagers, who gather around the fire. The noise follows an irregular rhythm, sometimes reverberating, sometimes murmuring. At times the rain is almost a gentle drizzle, at others it's a deluge whose hammering foreshadows some disaster. Broken branches litter the ground.

I return and dry myself off. The shack is quiet. I go straight into Petit Loko's room. I lie down on the mat with my weapon at my side. I'm naked in the dark. Inside a house where ants, flies, and mosquitoes usually keep us from a good rest, I sleep for several hours on end. I awake with a start. Petit Loko has returned and is stumbling into everything. He falls on me in a heap and jumps when he comes into contact with me, reacting angrily. "Hey, who's there?"

I whisper some incomprehensible words.

"Oh, it's you? Are you cold? Well, what are you doing there? If my father knew that you've come here, he'd kill you!"

"Don't worry about it. Pa Loko will never know. He's fast asleep."

"You know there's no shortage of venomous tongues around here. I've been discreet up till now. After all, he's my father, and I don't know if he'd give me his blessing. Ever since my mother disappeared, he's been in a bad temper."

"I'm discreet. Tonight I want you to take me like when you caught me behind the manioc fields. And anyway, it's raining so hard that no one will hear a thing. For the first time, we'll do it on a mat like a real couple. Come here, I want you."

I tell him that I need to go fetch the lamp all the same. It's too dark. Without the light, I won't see his face when he groans with pleasure.

Actually, I'm afraid of sticking the arrow just anywhere. In the lamplight, I'll have a better chance of enjoying his pain. Evil is on my side this time. With Petit Loko, I'll start with the penis, which will be displayed on the village square. Everyone will bear witness to the instruments of my torture.

The younger Loko turns toward me abruptly. I'm completely naked on the mat. My body isn't trembling; I'm made of wood.

"Hey, your breasts have sprouted since last time. Soon, all the swine in the village will want to touch them. Let me look at them. Like lemons, you'd say. Well then, our little girl is growing up!"

He presses hard on my left breast. I don't give him an opportunity to continue. Gazing at the ceiling, I see Sita Ndomè who's looking at me tenderly. Same smile, same look, same gestures. With a twist of the wrist, I jab the arrow into his buttock. Another blow hits his leg. It's a clean blow, a direct hit. The boy's yelling so loudly that the neighbors should hear, but everything is muffled by the clamor of the rain, now my objective ally. It falls, sonorous and musical. I wrench out the arrow and thrust it into his stomach, then the other leg, then the other buttock. I thrust and wrench, thrust and wrench. I repeat the blows for a minute. Petit, otherwise known as Muna Loko, is literally pissing blood. He screams like a steer at the slaughterhouse. Unlike his father, his cries are more vigorous. In one swift blow, I cut off his penis. A pool of hemoglobin forms. Petit Muna Loko's eyes go out . . .

I leave the house and let the rain wash me for a long time. I feel a strange sense of tranquility. Even under the deluge, the village seems calm. I realize that I'm also a link in that cursed line of descendants, the Lokos. Washed clean by the cascade, I return to my bed and for the first time pass a very pleasant night's rest. My act has totally transformed me. From then on I sleep without being awoken by nightmares.

The morning is fresh. The rain is still falling, light and constant.

I leave the house and head to the neighbors' to tell them I've finally avenged myself. I run to the manager of *Bon pour tous* and present her the three penises tied up in a red scarf, a fatal packet of what the village left unsaid. No child will be raped in Mpongo anymore. Domestic violence will henceforth be exposed, to the great shame of the perverse souls.

When she sees me, the owner of the bistro starts yelling her head off.

"Madame, calm down! These three penises are the mark of my life!"

The nice woman knew all the details, but she'd kept quiet, like everyone else. Never mind that. With this evidence, I reveal the original version. I take the time to explain everything to her. She suspected that a curse would strike the village one day, and that Mota Loko had taken me as his wife. Then I tell her that I murdered the Lokos, father and son, as well as Sango Kouta. Eventually she can't take it anymore. She shrieks loudly, which brings people running. They're faced with three bodies, I mean three men with detached pieces.

Certain portions I throw to the dogs, who wolf them down. Now they've become partners in my revenge, which delights me. No one feeds those poor beasts. Today is a feast day for them. And at the heart of the feast are those penises detached from their owners, anonymous penises, since no one can identify which is which. They all look like bits of bloody sausage. I'm wearing the red dress that the real owner of *Bon pour tous* gave me after I was first raped. May she rest in peace. I want to honor her memory. I know she's proud of me.

V

I leave the village and walk straight ahead.

To tell the truth, I don't know where I'm going. I've heard of busses that go to the big city, but I don't have any money. I go there anyway. When I arrive at the station, a bus is next in line to leave. People get on and off as they await its departure. They mill about, hail each other, shout. They're hotly discussing the scandal that took place the previous day in Mpongo. "The bodies of Sango Kouta, Mota Loko, and his son called Petit Muna Loko were found this morning. All three of them killed by the little orphan who doesn't even have a name," bellows one traveler.

The driver laughs nervously. His eyes are shining. "Oh, those villagers! What stories they tell!" he exclaims. "People love sordid gossip," he continues. "How could an adolescent girl kill three men at once? And all by herself. Were those three victims real men or what? No, it's impossible! Or else God wanted them to die. Those guys deserved to die, then. Among our people, the Duala, you don't touch children. A child is sacred." And with that he concludes his monologue of sorts.

The driver's remarks don't do any good. Tongues are still wagging on every side. People are on the lookout for the goriest version of the events.

I timidly approach the driver, who's going to leave the station soon, and confide to him, "I'm the criminal. I killed them, those nasty rapists, but I don't have anywhere to go. I just want to get far away from here."

"Sit down and keep quiet. As you can see, the only thing they're talking about is your story," he tells me in confidence.

In Douala, the largest city in Cameroon, the driver takes me to the house of his mistress, who adopts me at once. She needs some help with her housework. She sells makala ma mbasi and teaches me how to fry them. The woman lives in a single room. I sleep on the floor in the corner. She never yells at me and gently explains to me how things work here. "In life, you have to do what you can to survive," she advises.

One day, she compliments me. "You've gained weight. You'll be a pretty young girl." She's happy and smiles. The compliment actually marks the beginning of another misfortune. A few months later, we discover that I'm pregnant. And I'm only fourteen years old!

In these times of distress, Sita Ndomè is the only édimo I gaze at, whether she appears in the clouds or on the ceiling. She never abandons me. She suspected my situation and took measures for me to abort. Every night before going to bed, I drink a certain amount of yellowish liquid. As I'm lying on my mat, Sita appears and encourages me to drink up at all costs. The beverage is bitter and reeks to boot. All week Sita watches to make sure I comply. A few days later, I lose the child without any harm to my health. The next month, pains in my stomach arise which develop into a hemorrhage. My guardian explains that this blood bears witness to the start of a new life for me. I'm taken to the hospital where they clean out my uterus. My new existence begins. I decide to set up my own business then. To repay my hostess for her kindness, Sita the fairy grants her most cherished wish. My guardian has been wanting a child with her lover the driver, but she hasn't been able to conceive. And contrary to all expectation, here she is expecting a child! Her pregnancy passes without a problem, and a beautiful child is born.

VI

What does it feel like to sleep with a woman who killed three men at once? Nothing much in particular, since she seduced me with her voice, her body, her breasts, which now all give me pleasure in the most unexpected ways. Not only would I dismiss any future doubt about her innocence, but I also would never give in to any remorse that would lead me to denounce her to the police. Panè didn't kill, she never committed murder. She's the star who, from the heights of the heavens, shines down. She reveals the human cowardice that gives rise to an intolerable tolerance for criminals. With Panè, I live an exceptional love.

The first time she invited me to her house, she welcomed me on these terms, "I have a modest home, two poufs and a mat right on the floor. No table or chairs, I don't see the use."

So we sat on the poufs eating grilled seasoned fish with boiled plantain.

Clouds cover the sky. It's going to rain. The inhabitants of Bona Mbella gather together. The children are cheerful, linger in the streets. No sign of sadness hangs over our heads. People breathe . . . We contemplate them . . .

Behind closed doors, I tremble with desire. In Panè's eyes, I see the reflection of my own. She gets up suddenly and gives me a kiss on my forehead. I hold out my hand to her, and she kisses it gently as well. We spend the night cuddling each other and telling each other little stories, as close as two halves of the same brain. Like children, we interlace inside the same spiritual body . . .

It's dark in the room, and I turn on the light to look at her body, blazing from the red muslin surrounding it. I'm dazzled. My hands follow the contours of her buttocks, her stomach, her thighs, her pointed breasts, her shoulders. I caress the other shoulder, the one with the tattoo, and place a few kisses on the little bird. I feel Panè opening beneath my fingers like a flower. She sings my name in two tones. "*Chan Tou. Chan Tou. Chan Tou.*" The moment when she caves in with pleasure is when I suck her toes. I take them in my mouth one by one to make the pleasure last. Panè moves in languid slow motion. She looks at me with an intensity that disturbs me. In comparison, I prefer the sounds that originate from her throat, melodies in which I melt like hot chocolate.

The rising dawn saddens me a little since I like to sleep in. But from the cock's first crow, Panè gets ready for her makala ma mbasi. The whole neighborhood is dreaming about them. And through the half-open window I sigh after my early morning Venus.

ACKNOWLEDGMENTS

I would like to thank Emily Goedde for her help editing the translation with a keen eye and a sensitive ear.

BIBLIOGRAPHY

Diabate, Naminata. "From Women Loving Women in Africa to Jean Genet and Race: A Conversation with Frieda Ekotto." *Journal of the African Literature Association (JALA)* 4, no. 1 (2009): 181–203.

———. "Genealogies of Desire, Extravagance, and Radical Queerness in Frieda Ekotto's *Chuchote Pas Trop.*" *Research in African Literatures* 47, no. 2 (2016): 46–65.

Ekotto, Frieda. *Race and Sex across the French Atlantic: The Color of Black in Literary, Philosophical, and Theater Discourse.* Massachusetts: Lexington Press, 2011.

———. "Framing Homosexual Identities in Cameroonian Literature." *Tydskrif vir Letterkunde (Journal for Literature)* 53, no. 1 (2016): 128–37.

———. "Why Do We Always Say Nothing?" Paper delivered at the Modern Language Association Convention Boston, MA, January 2013.

Ellerson, Beti. Interview. "Frieda Ekotto: For an Endogenous Critique of Representations of African Lesbian Identity in Visual Culture and Literature." *African Women in Cinema Blog.* November 13, 2013. http://africanwomenincinema.blogspot.com/2013/11/frieda-ekotto -for-endogenous-critique.html (accessed November 27, 2015).

Gordon, Avery F. *Ghostly Matters: Haunting and the Sociological Imagination.* 2nd ed. Minneapolis: University of Minnesota Press, 2008.

ABOUT THE AUTHOR

Frieda Ekotto is Chair of the Department of Afroamerican and African Studies and Professor of Comparative Literature at the University of Michigan. Her early work involves an interdisciplinary exploration of the interactions among philosophy, law, literature, and African cinema. Her most recent book is titled *Race and Sex across the French Atlantic: The Color of Black in Literary, Philosophical, and Theater Discourse* (Lexington Press, 2011).

ABOUT THE TRANSLATOR

Corine Tachtiris translates literature primarily by contemporary women authors from Africa, the Caribbean, and the Czech Republic. She holds an MFA in literary translation from the University of Iowa and a PhD in comparative literature from the University of Michigan. She teaches world literature and translation theory and practice.